THE SUFFERINGS
OF
YOUNG WERTHER

Johann Wolfgang von Goethe

THE SUFFERINGS
OF
YOUNG WERTHER

Translated by

HARRY STEINHAUER
UNIVERSITY OF CALIFORNIA, SANTA BARBARA

W · W · NORTON & COMPANY

New York · London

W. W. Norton & Company, Inc., 500 Fifth Avenue, New York, N.Y. 10110

ISBN 0-393-09880-4

Library of Congress Catalog Card No. 70-95519
Printed in the United States of America

6 7 8 9 0

Contents

Preface

In his treatise on Goethe's *Elective Affinities* the late Walter Benjamin drew a distinction between the "factual content" of a literary work and its "truth content." A great work of literature is one in which both elements coalesce to form a perfect whole. But Benjamin recognized that, with the passing of time, the congruence wears off, the two types of content come apart, so that even the work which preserves its truth content raises problems with regard to its factual content. Stated less abstrusely, this distinction takes cognizance of the fact that Homer or the authors of Genesis are relevant to us in the twentieth century in the interpretation of life which they present, even though their way of presenting truth is no longer our way. Nor is Goethe's. That is why it is necessary to retranslate Homer, the Bible, and Goethe repeatedly. And the translator is faced with the task of providing a version for the reader of today in our idiom and yet remaining faithful to the spirit of the original.

It is principally matters affecting customs, fashion, etiquette, forms of address, and politeness that resist translation into the idiom of our time. The men of the eighteenth century wept to indicate heightened emotion; Werther wets Lotte's hand "with a thousand tears." His letters are profuse in exclamations of "woe" and "alas," for which we have no equivalent in our hard-boiled world of today. He repeatedly apostrophizes his correspondent as "dear friend," "dearest friend," or "brother." Rather than omit these "factual truths," I have preferred to include them as reminders to the reader that he is dealing with a book that was written in the sentimental age. For the same reason I have at times translated the German word *Seele* with the English *soul*, although in most cases I have offered our modern secular equivalents, as I understand them. I have also followed the rather loose syntax into which Werther lapses during his moments of excitement—the letter of May 10 or the last letter of Book One. But I have toned down much that would strike the modern reader as maudlin, though it somehow sounds right in Goethe's German.

I wish to express my gratitude to my colleague, Professor Rolf Linn, who was always willing to spend time wrangling with me over the precise translation of a single word, and to Mrs. Connie Hodge and Mrs. Karin Arvis for their help in preparing the manuscript for the press.

HARRY STEINHAUER

THE SUFFERINGS
OF
YOUNG WERTHER

*Whatever I have been able to discover about the story of poor
Werther, I have collected with diligence, and I place it before you,
and I know you will thank me for it. You cannot withhold your
admiration or your love from his spirit and character, nor your
tears from his fate.*

*And you, good soul, who feel the same anguish as he, derive
comfort from his sufferings, and let this little book be your friend,
if your destiny or your own fault should prevent you from finding
a more intimate one.*

Book One

How glad I am that I got away! Dearest friend, what a thing is
the heart of man! To leave you whom I love so much, from whom
I was inseparable, and yet be glad! I know you will forgive me.
Were not my other attachments deliberately designed by fate to
torment a heart like mine? Poor Leonore![1] And yet I was not to
blame. Could I help it that, while her sister's wayward charms provided me with pleasant entertainment, a passion for me grew in her
unfortunate heart? And yet, am I wholly without blame? Didn't I
encourage her emotions? Didn't I find delight in the wholly sincere
expressions of nature which so often made us laugh, however little
there was to laugh at? Didn't I—oh, what is man, that he dare
reproach himself! I will, my dear friend, I promise you, I will
improve; I will no longer, as I have always done, ruminate on the
scrap of misfortune that destiny serves up to us; I will enjoy the
present, and the past shall be past for me. Of course you are right,
my dear friend, there would be less suffering among men if they
did not—God knows why they are so constituted—expend so much
zeal and imagination in recalling the memory of past ills, instead of
enduring an indifferent present.

Will you be good enough to tell my mother that I will look after
her business as best I can and report to her about it as soon as possible. I spoke to my aunt and found her anything but the disagreeable person we make of her at home. She is a lively, impetuous
woman with the best of hearts. I explained to her my mother's
complaints about the portion of the inheritance that has been
withheld from her; she gave me her grounds, reasons, and the conditions under which she would be prepared to give up everything,
even more than we asked. —In short, I don't want to write about
the matter now; tell mother that everything will come out all right.
And, my dear friend, I have found once again in this little affair

1. Lenore plays the same role in this
novel as Rosaline in Shakespeare's
Romeo and Juliet: she is the object of
a former superficial love, in contrast to
the deep love to come.

1

that misunderstandings and indolence perhaps cause more error in the world than cunning and malice. At least, the latter two are certainly rarer. For the rest, I feel very comfortable here. The solitude in this heavenly region is a precious balm for my heart, and this youthful season warms my often shivering heart with all its abundance. Every tree, every hedge, is a bouquet of blossoms; and one would like to turn into a June bug, to be able to float upon this sea of perfume and find all one's nourishment in it.

The town itself is disagreeable, but the surrounding country has an inexpressible natural beauty. That is why the late Count von M—— was induced to lay out a garden on one of the hills which cross each other in the most beautiful variety and form the loveliest valleys. The garden is simple, and the moment you enter it you feel that it was planned, not by a scientific gardener[2] but by a feeling heart which wished to find enjoyment here. I have already shed many a tear for the deceased in the dilapidated cottage which was his favorite spot and is mine too. I shall soon be master of the garden; the gardener has become attached to me in these few days I've been here, and he will not regret it.

May 10

A wonderful serenity has taken possession of my whole soul, like the sweet spring mornings which I enjoy with all my heart. I am alone and am savoring my life in this region, which was made just for souls such as mine. I am so happy, my dear friend, so completely absorbed by the feeling of peaceful existence, that my art is suffering. I couldn't draw now, not a line, and yet I have never been a greater painter than I am in these moments.[3] When the lovely valley around me is shrouded in mist, and the high sun rests on the impenetrable darkness of my forest, and only single rays steal into the inner sanctuary,[4] I then lie in the tall grass beside the cascading brook, and close to the ground a thousand varieties of tiny grasses fill me with wonder; when I feel this teeming little

2. The world of the *Sturm und Drang* is revealed here in the preference for the natural or "English" garden over the geometrically-pruned "French" garden of the baroque period; in the contrast between the intellect and the heart; in the cult of ruins (the dilapidated cottage); in the tears which Werther sheds so frequently.
3. An echo of Conti's speech in *Emilia Galotti*. Cf. Afterword, pp. 112-113.
4. In Herder's circle the syntactical structure of the following period was known as "the homiletic order of battle" (*die homiletische Schlachtordnung*). It goes back to an ancient tradition in rhetoric and was popular in sermons and theological writing. It consists of a series of parallel conditional clauses, increasing in emotional intensity, followed by a pause and a declining cadence. The religious provenance of the figure has left its mark on Werther's sentence.

world among the stalks closer to my heart—the countless, unfathomable forms of tiny worms and gnats—and feel the presence of the Almighty, who created us in His image, the breath of the All-loving One who, floating in eternal bliss, bears and sustains us; my friend, when my eyes then grow misty[5] and the world about me and the sky dwell wholly within me like the form of a beloved woman—then I often think with longing: oh, if you could express this once more, if you could breathe onto the paper what lives so fully, so warmly within you, so that it might become the mirror of your soul, as your soul is the mirror of infinite[6] God!—My friend—but this will destroy me, I am overwhelmed by the power of these glorious visions.

May 12

I don't know whether deceptive spirits hover about this region or whether it is the warm, heavenly fantasies in my heart that transform everything about me into such a paradise. Just outside the town there is a spring, a spring which holds me in its spell like Melusine[7] and her sisters. You go down a little hill and find yourself in front of an arch; about twenty steps lead down to a spot where the clearest water flows from marble rocks. The little wall forms the enclosure above, the tall trees which shade it all around, the coolness of the spot—all this has something so attractive, so thrilling about it. Not a day passes that I do not spend an hour sitting there. The girls come from the town to fetch water, that most innocent and most necessary business, which at one time the daughters of kings performed themselves. When I sit there, the patriarchial idea is so vividly alive about me; I see how they, all those patriarchs, become acquainted and do their courting at the well,[8] and how beneficent spirits hover over wells and springs. Oh, the man who cannot feel this with me can never have taken comfort from the coolness of a spring after a hard day of summer walking.

May 13

You ask whether you should send me my books—my dear friend, I beg you, in the name of Heaven, don't saddle me with them! I don't want to be guided, encouraged, inspired any more, for this heart is surging enough by itself. I need lullabies, and these I have

---

5. *Dämmern*, a favorite word of the *Sturm und Drang*, more "romantic" than the full light, which is a symbol of consciousness and intellect.

6. *Unendlich*, another romantic word, expressing the urge to transcend the limitations of this existence.

7. Melusine, the legendary mermaid who married a mortal. Her story is told in a chapbook.

8. An allusion to Genesis 24 and 29. The German word *Brunnen* means both well and spring.

found in abundance in my Homer.[9] How often do I lull my seething blood to rest, for you have never seen anything so uneven, so unsteady as this heart. Dear friend! Need I tell this to you, who have so often borne the burden of seeing me pass from grief to wild exuberance and from sweet melancholy to destructive passion? Moreover, I coddle my precious heart like a sick child; I grant its every wish. Don't tell this to anyone; there are people who would resent it.

May 15

The common people of the place already know me and love me, especially the children.[1] When I first sought their company and asked them in a friendly way about this and that, some of them thought I wanted to make fun of them and even brushed me off rudely. I didn't mind this; only I felt most keenly what I have often noticed before: that people of some social position will always keep a cold distance from the common folk as though they thought they would lose something by closer contact; and then there are shallow minds and evil-minded pranksters who appear to condescend, just to make the poor people feel their arrogance the more keenly.

I know quite well that we are not and cannot be equal; but I believe that the man who thinks it necessary to keep himself aloof from the so-called mob in order to maintain their respect is as much to blame as a coward who hides from his enemy because he is afraid of being defeated.

Recently I went to the spring and found a young servant girl who had set her pitcher on the lowest step and was looking around to see if some other girl might be coming to help her place it on her head. I went down and looked at her. "Shall I help you, Miss?" I said —Her face turned a deep red. —"Oh no, sir," she said. —"It's a trifle." —She adjusted her headpiece[2] and I helped her. She thanked me and walked up the steps.

May 17

I have made all sorts of acquaintances, but have found no true companions yet. I don't know what the attraction is that I have for

---

9. Homer, symbol of simplicity and the naïve (Rousseau's "nature"), which to the "sentimental" man connotes happiness.
1. The simple folk and children are symbols of Rousseauistic "nature."
2. *Kringen*, a cushion of cloth, stuffed with horsehair, to soften the weight of the load borne on the head.

people; so many of them like me and attach themselves to me, and then it hurts me when we can only travel a short stretch on the same road. If you ask me what the people here are like, I must tell you—like people everywhere. The human race is a pretty uniform commodity. Most people work away the greater part of their time earning a living, and the little freedom they have left causes them such anxiety, that they ferret out every means of getting rid of it.[3] Oh, destiny of man!

But they really are a decent sort of people. When I occasionally forget myself, and share with them the pleasures that are still left to man, such as enjoying myself in frankness and sincerity at a well-stocked table, arranging an excursion or dance at the right time, and so on, the effect on me is quite salutary; but I must not be reminded that so many other forces lie dormant within me, atrophying for lack of use, and which I must carefully conceal. Oh, how that constricts my heart! —And yet, to be misunderstood is the fate of a man like myself.

Alas, that the friend[4] of my youth is gone. Alas, that I ever knew her! —I would say: You're a fool; you are looking for what cannot be found down here; but I did possess her friendship, I did feel the warmth of her heart, her noble soul, in whose presence I seemed to be more in my own eyes than I really was, because I was everything I could be. Good Heavens! Was there any faculty of my mind that was idle? Could I not unfold before her the whole marvelous feeling with which my heart embraces nature? Was our association not an endless stirring of the most delicate feeling, the keenest wit, the nuances of which were all stamped with the mark of genius[5] to the point of extravagance? And now! —Alas, the years she had in advance of me led her to the grave before me. Never shall I forget her, never her resolute mind and her divine patience.

A few days ago I met a young man, V——, a frank lad with most pleasing features. He has just left the university, doesn't exactly consider himself wise, but still believes that he knows more than other people. He worked, too, for which I have all sorts of evidence; in short, he is quite well informed. When he heard that I do a lot of sketching and know Greek (two unusual phenomena in this part of the country), he came to me and unloaded much learn-

3. This passage anticipates the central thesis of Erich Fromm's book *Escape from Freedom.*
4. An older woman who acted as a spiritual mentor to Werther (cf. page 89), as Susanne von Klettenberg did to the young Goethe. Such mentors of either sex were common in the life and literature of the eighteenth century.
5. *Genie*, one of the key words of the *Sturm und Drang,* also known as the *Genieperiode* because it glorified genius—i.e., deep emotion or wild inspiration over dull regularity.

ing,[6] from Batteux to Wood, from De Piles to Winckelmann, and assured me that he had read through the entire first part of Sulzer's *Theory*, and possessed a manuscript by Heyne on the study of classical antiquity. I paid no heed to him. I've made the acquaintance of another very nice person, the Prince's magistrate, a candid, sincere man. I hear it is a joy to see him among his children—he has nine; they mention especially his oldest daughter. He invited me to his home and I will visit him very soon. He lives in one of the Prince's hunting lodges, an hour and a half from here, which he was permitted to occupy after the death of his wife, since it was too painful for him to live on here in town at his official residence.

Apart from that, I have crossed paths with some eccentric characters whom I find altogether intolerable, most of all in their demonstrations of friendship. Good-by! You will like this letter; it's quite factual.

May 22

That the life of man is but a dream has been felt by many a man before me, and this feeling attends me constantly, too. When I observe the limited sphere within which man's active and contemplative faculties are pent up; when I see how all our activity merely serves to satisfy needs which in turn serve no other purpose than to prolong our wretched existence; and then realize that our equanimity concerning certain points of inquiry is only a dreamy resignation in which we decorate the walls of our prison with colored figures and bright views—all this, Wilhelm, robs me of my speech. I turn back upon myself and find a world! But again, more in imagination and obscure desire than in actuality and living power. And so everything swims before my senses, and I smile my way dreamily through the world.

All the highly learned schoolmasters, public and private, are agreed that children don't know why they want something; but that adults, too, like children, stumble about on this earth of ours

---

6. Werther's contempt for theory is characteristic of the romantic revolt against the *Aufklärung*. Charles Batteux (1713–1780), French writer on aesthetics, author of *Les beaux arts réduits à un même principe*. Robert Wood (1717–1775), Scottish archaeologist, author of *Essay on the Original Genius and Writings of Homer*. Roger de Piles (1635–1709), painter, and writer on aesthetics, author of *Abrégé de la vie des peintres*. Johann Joachim Winckelmann (1717–1768), archaeologist, art historian, one of the great minds of the eighteenth century. Johann Georg Sulzer (1720–1779), author of a much read encyclopedia of art, *Theorie der schönen Künste* (1774). Christian Heyne (1729–1812), philologist, professor at the University of Göttingen. The "manuscript" is a set of unpublished lecture notes.

and do not know where they come from or where they are going; that their behavior is guided just as little by true purpose and governed just as much by biscuits and cake and the birch rod—no one wants to believe this, and yet, it seems to me that it is palpably so. I'll gladly admit—for I know what you would like to say to me—that those people are happiest who live but for the day, the way children do, who drag their dolls about, dress and undress them, respectfully circle the drawer in which mother has locked the cookies, and when they finally get what they want, stuff it into their mouths and cry, "More!" —They are happy creatures. They are happy, too, who give pompous titles to their shabby occupations, or even to their passions, and represent them as gigantic operations for the salvation and welfare of the human race. —Happy the man who can be like that! But he who, in his humility, recognizes what all this amounts to, he who sees how nicely every comfortable citizen can trim his little garden into a paradise, and how patiently even the unhappy man struggles on his way beneath his burden, and how everyone is equally interested in beholding the light of this sun for just one more minute—yes, such a person is serene and creates his world out of himself and is even happy to be a human being. And however circumscribed he may be, he always preserves in his heart the sweet feeling of freedom and the knowledge that he can leave this prison whenever he wants to.

May 26

You have long known my habit of sinking roots, putting up a cottage[7] in some cozy place and settling in it in spite of its limitations. Here, too, I have found a little spot which has attracted me.

About an hour's distance from town there is a place called Wahlheim.[8] It has a very interesting[9] situation on a hill, and when you leave the village by the upper footpath, you suddenly look out over the whole valley. The hostess at the inn, a pleasant and cheerful good woman in her old age, dispenses wine, beer, and coffee; but the principal attraction is the two linden trees which spread their ample boughs over the little square in front of the church; the square is enclosed by peasant cottages, barns, and farmyards. I have

7. *Hüttchen*, a favorite word of the time, symbolizing idyllic bliss in nature. Goethe used it frequently in his *Sturm und Drang* period.
8. The reader need not trouble to seek the places named here; it has been necessary to change the names in the original letters [Goethe's note].
9. *Interessant*, another characteristic "period" word, like "picturesque," associated with the new romantic feeling. Cf. page 8, line 15. In modern usage the word has lost the vivid tone it had for the later eighteenth century.

rarely found a spot that is so intimate and cozy; I have my little table and chair brought out from the inn, drink my coffee and read my Homer there. The first time I came by chance upon the linden trees on a beautiful afternoon, I found the little square quite deserted. Everybody was out in the fields; the only one present was a boy about four years old, who was sitting on the ground, holding between his feet another child of about six months, whom he pressed against his chest with both arms so that he formed a sort of armchair for the infant; in spite of the merriment that danced in his black eyes as he looked about him, he sat quite still. The sight pleased me; I sat down on a plow which stood across from them and made a sketch of the brotherly scene with great delight. I added the nearby hedge, a barn door, and some broken wagon wheels, exactly as they lay there; and after an hour had passed I found that I had made a very interesting and well-arranged drawing, without adding anything of my own to it. This confirmed me in my resolution to keep exclusively to nature[1] in the future. She alone is infinitely rich and she alone forms the great artist. You can say much for rules, about as much as may be said in praise of bourgeois society. A person who models himself on them will never produce anything bad or in poor taste, just as a man who allows himself to be molded by convention and decorum can never become an unbearable neighbor or a notorious villain; on the other hand, say what you will, all rules destroy a true feeling for nature and its true expression. You will say this is too harsh, the rule merely restrains, prunes the rank growth of the vine, etc. —Dear friend, shall I give you an analogy? It's like love. A young fellow is wholly attached to a girl, spends every hour of the day with her, squanders all his energy, his whole fortune, in order to express to her at every moment that he is completely devoted to her. And then along comes a philistine,[2] a man who holds a public office, and says to him: "My dear young man, to love is human, but you must love within human bounds. Divide up your hours; use some for work and set aside your leisure hours for your girl. Assess your fortune; I don't forbid you to give her a present from what is left to you after you have taken care of the necessities, but not too often, say for her birthday or saint's day, etc." If he follows this advice, you will have a useful young man, and I myself would advise every prince to make him a member of his government; but it's all up with his love, and if he is an artist, with his art too. Oh, my friends! Why

1. The conflict between nature and the "rules" is central in the rise of romantic sensibility.

2. *Philister*, Philistine, Babbitt, "square": the smug, conventional opponent of culture.

does the torrent of genius burst forth so rarely, so seldom roar in high waves and shake you to the depths of your astonished souls? —Dear friends, there on both sides of the river, live unruffled gentlemen; their little summerhouses, tulip beds, and vegetable gardens would be ruined; they are, therefore, able to avert the threatening danger by building dams and ditches.

May 27

I see I have fallen into raptures, parables, and declamation and have forgotten in the process to complete my story about the children. I had been sitting on my plow for about two hours, completely absorbed in artistic contemplation, which my letter of yesterday shows you in a very fragmentary manner. Then, toward evening, a young woman with a little basket on her arm came up to the children, who had not stirred all this time, and called from a distance: "Philip, you're a real good boy." —She greeted me, I thanked her, stood up, went over to her, and asked her if she was the mother of the children. She said yes and, giving the older child half a roll, she lifted up the baby and kissed it with all of a mother's love. —"I gave Philip the baby to hold," she said, "and went into town with my oldest boy to get white bread, sugar, and an earthen dish for his cereal." I saw all these items in the basket, from which the cover had fallen. "I want to cook some soup for my Hans (that was the name of the youngest) for his supper; that rascal, the big one, broke the dish yesterday when he was quarreling with Philip about the scrapings of the cereal." I asked her about her oldest; she had scarcely finished telling me that he was chasing a few geese on the meadow when he came running up, bringing Philip a hazel switch. I went on talking with the woman and learned that she was the daughter of the schoolmaster and that her husband had gone to Switzerland to collect the inheritance left to him by a cousin. "They wanted to cheat him out of it," she said, "and didn't answer his letters; so he has gone there himself. I only hope he hasn't met with an accident; I've heard nothing from him." I found it difficult to tear myself away from the woman. I gave each of the children a penny and I gave her one for the youngest too, so that she could bring him a roll for his soup when she next went to town; and so we parted.

I tell you, my dear friend, when my senses are on the point of failing me, all my inner turmoil is relieved by the sight of such a creature, moving in happy tranquility within the narrow sphere of her existence, living from one day to the next; when she sees the leaves falling, she has no other thought than that winter is coming.

Since that time I have been out there often. The children are quite used to me; they get sugar when I drink my coffee, and in the evening they share my bread and butter and my sour milk. On Sundays they never fail to get their pennies, and if I am not there after the church service, the landlady has orders to pay them.

I have their confidence, they tell me all sorts of things, and I find special delight in their passions and naïve outbursts of desire when their village children gather.

It was a great effort for me to relieve the mother of the anxiety that they might "inconvenience[3] the gentleman."

May 30

What I told you recently about painting is certainly true of literature too. The point is that one should recognize what is excellent and dare express it, and that is, of course, saying a great deal in a few words. I experienced a scene today which would yield the most beautiful idyll in the world if it could be told accurately; but why talk of poetry, scene, idyll? Must we be eternally tinkering when we are to experience a natural phenomenon?

If you expect a lot of elevated and noble thoughts after this introduction, you will be badly deceived again; it is only a peasant lad who has moved me to feel this lively sympathy. I'll tell my story badly, as usual, and as usual you will find that I exaggerate. It is Wahlheim again, always Wahlheim, that produces these extraordinary states in me.

There was a group outside under the linden trees drinking coffee. Because the company did not quite suit me, I stayed inside under some pretext.

A farm boy came out of a nearby house and got busy repairing the plow which I had recently sketched.[4] Because I liked his manner, I spoke to him and inquired about his circumstances. We were soon acquainted and, as usually happens to me with people of that sort, soon on familiar terms. He told me that he was in the service of a widow who was treating him well. He talked about her

---

3. The German text has *inkommodie-ren*, a French word. The foreign word suggests the deference which the simple woman feels toward the "gentleman." Margarete, the heroine of *Faust*, stands in the same relationship to her admirer as the simple woman of this novel does to Werther. She uses the same deferential word when Faust kisses her hand:

"Inkommodiert Euch nicht. Wie könnt Ihr sie mir küssen?" (Do not incommode yourself. How can you possibly kiss it? [*Faust*, line 3081]).

4. On page 8, line 11 we are told that Werther was sitting on the plow while he sketched. This letter was not in the first version of *Werther*.

so much and praised her so warmly that I could see he had a deep affection for her. She was no longer young, he said. She had been badly treated by her first husband and refused to marry again; his words showed so clearly how beautiful, how charming he found her, how very much he wished that she might choose him to erase the memory of her first husband's failings, that I would have to report word for word what he said if I wanted to give you a vivid picture of this man's pure affection, love, and faithfulness. In fact, I would have to possess the gifts of the greatest poet to convey to you adequately his expressive gestures, his harmonious voice, the hidden fire in his eyes. No, words cannot express the tenderness that was in his whole being and expression; everything that I could reproduce here would be merely crude. I was especially touched by his apprehension that I might wrongly interpret his relationship to her and doubt the propriety of her conduct. How charming it was when he spoke of her figure, her body, which drew him to her and held him captive although it lacked the graces of youth, I can only repeat to myself in my inmost being. Never in my life have I seen intense longing and ardent desire in such purity; indeed, I might say I have never thought or dreamed it could exist in such purity. Don't scold me if I tell you that my very soul glows at the memory of this innocence and truth, and that the image of this fidelity and tenderness pursues me everywhere, and that I pine and languish as though kindled by it myself.

I will now try to see her too, as soon as I can; or rather, on second thought, I will try to avoid such an encounter. It is better if I see her through the eyes of her lover; perhaps she will not look the way she now stands before me, and why should I spoil the lovely image?

June 16

Why don't I write to you? —You ask that and yet you are one of the sages. You should be able to guess that I am well, and, in fact—in short, I have met someone who touches my heart closely. I have—I don't know.

To tell you in a logical way how it came about that I met one of the most lovely creatures will be difficult. I am contented and happy, and so I can't be a good narrator.

An angel! —Nonsense! Every man says that about his girl, doesn't he? And yet I am unable to tell you how perfect she is, why she is perfect; enough, she has captivated all my senses.

So much simplicity with so much intelligence, so much kindness with so much firmness, and such tranquility of soul together with true life and activity.

All this I say about her is wretched nonsense, mere abstractions which do not express a single feature of her true self. Another time—no, not another time, I'll tell you about it right now. If I don't do it now, I never will. For between ourselves, since I began to write, I have been three times at the point of putting down my pen, having my horse saddled, and riding out to her. And yet I took an oath this morning not to ride out there; all the same, I go to my window every moment to see how high the sun still stands. I could not control myself, I had to go to her. Here I am again, Wilhelm, I'll have a slice of bread and butter for my supper and write you. How it rejoices my heart to see her in the circle of the dear, happy children, her eight brothers and sisters!—

If I continue like this, you will be no wiser in the end than you were in the beginning. So listen, I will force myself to give you details.

I wrote you recently how I made the acquaintance of Magistrate S——, and how he asked me to visit him soon in his hermitage, or rather his little kingdom. I neglected to do so and might perhaps never have gone if chance had not revealed to me the treasure that lies hidden in that quiet region.

The young people here had arranged a dance in the country, and I gladly agreed to attend. As my partner, I invited a girl from this town, nice, attractive, but otherwise insignificant, and it was arranged that I would hire a carriage and drive with my partner and her cousin to the scene of the festivities; on the way we were to pick up Charlotte S——. "You will meet a beautiful girl," said my companion as we drove through a clearing in the forest toward the hunting lodge. "Take care," the cousin added, "that you don't fall in love." "What do you mean?" I said. "She's already engaged," she replied, "to a very fine man, who is away on a trip to settle the estate of his father who died, and to apply for an important post." The information did not interest me much.

The sun was still a quarter of an hour above the hilltops when we drove up in front of the gate. It was very sultry and the women expressed concern about a storm that seemed to be gathering at the horizon in whitish-gray, heavy little clouds. I allayed their fear with a pretence to meteorological knowledge, although I myself began to fear that our entertainment would be upset.

I had gotten out of the carriage, and a maid who came to the gate asked us to wait a moment, Fräulein[5] Lotte would come at once. I walked through the courtyard to the well-built house, and

5. The German text has *Mamsell Lotte.* The use of the French word in eighteenth-century Germany by a ser- vant would indicate deference, perhaps also a touch of social pretension.

when I had gone up the front steps and entered the door, I was confronted by the most charming sight I have ever witnessed. In the entrance hall six children, from eleven to two years of age, were swarming about a girl with a beautiful figure, of medium height, who wore a simple white dress trimmed with pink bows at the arms and bosom. She was holding a loaf of dark bread, cutting for each of the little ones about her a slice in proportion to his age and appetite, gave each child his slice with such friendliness, and each cried his "Thank you" so artlessly, stretching out his little hands to her even before the slice had been cut, and then either hurried away contentedly with his supper or, if he was of a quieter temperament, walked away calmly toward the courtyard gate to see the strangers and the carriage in which their Lotte was to drive off. —"I beg your pardon," she said, "for troubling you to come in and for keeping the ladies waiting. But between dressing and giving all sorts of directions for the house while I am away, I forgot to give my children their supper, and they won't let anyone cut their bread for them except me." I paid her some insignificant compliment, but my whole mind was absorbed by the figure, the voice, the manner of the girl, and I just had time to recover from my surprise when she dashed into her room to fetch her gloves and fan. The young folk were giving me sidelong glances from a distance, and I walked up to the youngest one, a child with an adorable face. He drew back just as Lotte came out the door and said to him, "Louis, shake hands with your cousin." The boy did so very naturally, and I could not refrain from kissing him heartily in spite of his runny nose. "Cousin?" I said, as I offered my hand. "Do you think I deserve the good fortune of being related to you?" "Oh," she said with an animated smile, "we have a very extensive circle of cousins and I would be sorry if you were the worst among them." —As she left she instructed Sophie, a girl of about eleven and the oldest sister next to herself, to take good care of the children and to say hello to papa when he came home from his ride. She told the little ones to obey their sister Sophie as they would herself, which some of them definitely promised to do. But one saucy little blonde, about six years old, said: "But she isn't really you, Lotte, we really like you better." —The two oldest boys had climbed up behind the carriage and, at my request, she allowed them to ride with us to the edge of the forest if they promised not to tease each other and to hold on tight.

We had hardly settled in our seats, the ladies had welcomed each other, exchanged comments about each others' clothes, especially their hats, and made a due review of the company that was expected, when Lotte had the coachman stop and ordered her brothers to get down. They wanted to kiss her hand again, which the oldest one did with all the tenderness that can be characteristic of the age of fifteen, the other with much impetuousness and levity. She sent her love to the little children once more and we drove on.

The cousin asked whether she had finished the book she had recently sent her. "No," said Lotte, "I don't like it; you may have it back. The one I had before was no better." I was astonished when, upon asking what books they were, she replied:[6] —I found so much character in everything she said. With every word she uttered I saw new charms, new rays of intelligence flash from her features; which little by little seemed to take on a look of contentment because she felt that I understood her.

"When I was younger," she said, "I liked nothing so much as novels. Heaven knows how pleasant it was when I could sit down in a corner on Sunday and enter wholeheartedly into the good and bad fortune of some Miss Jenny.[7] And I do not deny that this type of reading still has some attraction for me. But since I so seldom get to read a book, it must really be to my taste. And the author I like best is the one in whose work I find my own world, the one who creates an environment like my own and whose story becomes as interesting and sympathetic as my own domestic existence, which is, to be sure, no paradise, but on the whole a source of boundless happiness."

I tried to conceal the emotion which these words aroused in me. But I fear my efforts were not very successful; for when I heard her talk casually, but with such truth, of *The Vicar of Wakefield*,[8] and of—,[9] I completely lost control of myself, told her everything that was on my mind, and noticed only after some time, when Lotte turned the conversation to the others, that they had been sitting there all this time, wide-eyed, as if they were not there. The cousin looked at me more than once with a mocking air, but I care little about that.

The conversation turned to the pleasure of dancing. "If this pas-

---

6. We feel obliged to suppress this passage in the letter, so that no one may be given cause for complaint. Although in reality, no author can be greatly concerned about the judgment of a single girl and an unstable young man [Goethe's note].

7. Allusion to either *Histoire de Miss Jenny Glanville* by Marie-Jeanne Riccoboni, which appeared in a German translation in 1764, or to the novel by J. T. Hermes, *Miss Fanny Wilkes* (1766), whose heroine is a Miss Jenny.

8. Oliver Goldsmith's *The Vicar of Wakefield* (1766) was popular in Germany soon after its appearance. Goethe was introduced to it by Herder in Strassburg; it remained a favorite throughout his life.

9. Here, too, the names of some native authors have been omitted. Those who share Lotte's approval will certainly feel in their hearts who they are when they get to this passage; others don't need to know [Goethe's note].

sion is a fault," said Lotte, "I will gladly confess to you that I know of nothing I value more. And if there is something on my mind, I pound out a quadrille on my out-of-tune piano and everything immediately is alright again."

How I feasted on those black eyes during the conversation, how those vivacious lips and those fresh, bright cheeks drew my whole being to her; how, completely absorbed in the delightful sound of her talk, I often did not hear the words in which she expressed herself!—you can have some idea of it, because you know me. In short, when we stopped in front of the pavilion, I got out of the carriage like a man in a dream and was so completely lost in dreams in the twilight world about me, that I scarcely heeded the music that echoed toward us from the brightly lit ballroom.

The two Messrs. Audran and a certain So and So—who can keep track of all the names?—who were the dancing partners of the cousin and Lotte, received us at the carriage door and took charge of their ladies, and I escorted mine upstairs.

We circled each other in minuets;[1] I led one lady after another, and it was precisely the most disagreeable women who could bring themselves to give me their hand and end the figure. Lotte and her partner began an English quadrille, and you can imagine how happy I felt when it was her turn to dance the figure with us. You should see her dance! Really, she is in it with all her heart and soul; her whole body is one harmony, so carefree, so natural, as though there were nothing else in life, as though she thought of nothing else, felt nothing else; and I'm sure that in such moments everything else vanishes before her.

I asked her for the second quadrille; she promised me the third, and assured me with the most charming frankness in the world that she loved to dance an *allemande*. "It's the fashion here," she continued, "that every couple belonging together remain together for the *allemande*, but my partner waltzes badly and will be grateful to me if I spare him the chore. Your lady can't dance it either and doesn't like to, but I saw during the quadrille that you waltz well; my escort and I will go to your lady." We shook hands on it and agreed that her partner should entertain mine in the meantime.

Then the dance began, and for a while we had fun interlacing our arms in various ways. With what charm, with what lightness she moved! And when we came to the waltz and the couples revolved about each other like the spheres, there was a bit of confusion at first, because only a very few knew how to do it. We were

---

1. The three types of dance mentioned here are: the French minuet, the English country or square dance, and the German waltz (*allemande*).

smart and let them wear themselves out, and when the clumsiest couples had cleared the floor, we sailed in and, together with another couple—Audran and his partner—held out bravely to the end. I've never felt so light on my feet. I was no longer a mortal. To hold the most charming creature in my arms and to fly around with her like a whirlwind, so that everything around me faded away, and—Wilhelm, to tell you the truth, I nevertheless took an oath that a girl I loved, on whom I had any claim, would never waltz with anyone besides myself, even if it meant my end. You know what I mean!

We took a few slow turns around the ballroom to recover our breath. Then she sat down, and the oranges I had put aside, the only ones now left, tasted wonderful, except that with every slice she politely offered to a greedy neighbor, I felt a stab in my heart.

In the third quadrille we were the second couple. As we were dancing through the ranks and I (Heaven knows with what bliss) clung to her arm and gazed into her eyes, which were filled with the sincerest expression of the frankest, purest pleasure, we reached a lady whose charming appearance had caught my attention, although her face was no longer young. She looked at Lotte with a smile, wagged a threatening finger at her as we whirled past, and spoke the name "Albert" twice, with much emphasis.

"Who is Albert," I said to Lotte, "if it is not impertinent to ask?" She was on the point of answering when we had to separate to form the big eight,[2] and it seemed to me her brow looked pensive as we crossed each other. "Why should I keep it from you?" she said, as she offered me her hand for the promenade. "Albert is a worthy man, to whom I'm as good as engaged." Now this was not news to me, for the girls had told me about it on the way, and yet it seemed new to me because I hadn't yet thought of it in relation to her, who had become so precious to me in a few moments. Enough—I became confused, lost my bearing, and got in with the wrong couple, so that everything was upside down, and it required all of Lotte's presence of mind, and some tugging and pulling, to put things quickly in order again.

The dance was not yet over when the lightning which we had seen flashing on the horizon for some time and which I had been explaining away as heat lightning, grew more intense, and the thunder drowned out the music. Three ladies left the ranks, followed by their escorts; the disorder became general and the music ceased. It is natural that, when a misfortune or some terrible event surprises us in a moment of pleasure, it should make a stronger impression

2. A figure in the square dance.

on us than at other times, partly because the contrast is so keenly
felt, partly and—this is more important—because our sensibility is
heightened and our senses are, therefore, more susceptible to an
impression. To these causes I must ascribe the strange grimaces
which I saw several ladies register. The most sensible one sat down
in a corner with her back to the window and held her hands over
her ears. Another knelt down before her and concealed her head in
the first girl's lap. A third pushed her way between them and threw
her arms about her companions with a thousand tears. Some
wanted to go home; others, who were even less aware of what they
were doing, lacked sufficient presence of mind to fend off the
impertinences of our young bloods, who seemed very busy trying to
steal the anxious prayers intended for Heaven from the lips of the
fair ladies in distress. Some of our gentlemen had gone downstairs
to smoke a pipe in peace; the rest of the company did not refuse
when the hostess hit upon the clever idea of showing us to a room
that had shutters and drapes. We had scarcely reached it when
Lotte got busy setting chairs in a circle and when, at her invitation,
the company had sat down, she proposed that we play a game.

I saw more than one man purse his lips and stretch his limbs in
anticipation of a juicy forfeit. "We'll play counting," said Lotte.
"Now pay attention. I'll go around the circle from right to left, and
you count off in turn, each saying the next number in the series,
and it must go like wildfire, and anyone who hesitates or makes a
mistake gets his ears boxed; and so on to a thousand". It was fun to
watch. She went around the circle with outstretched arm. "One,"
the first began, his neighbor said, "two," the next, "three," and so
on. Then she began to walk faster and faster; then someone missed,
and whack! a box on the ear. And amid the laughter the next man
too, whack! And faster still. I myself was slapped twice, and I
thought I noticed, with deep satisfaction, that she slapped me
harder than she did the others. General laughter and confusion
ended the game before we had reached a thousand. Groups of close
friends went off together; the storm was over and I followed Lotte
into the ballroom. On the way she said, "The slaps made them
forget the storm and everything else." —I was unable to say anything in reply. "I was one of the most anxious," she continued,
"and by pretending to be brave so as to inspire courage in the others, I did become brave." —We went to the window. There was
thunder off to one side, the glorious rain was pouring down over the
land, and the most refreshing fragrance rose up to us with the fullness of a warm breeze. She stood leaning on her elbows, her eyes
gazing out into the countryside; she looked up at the sky, and at me;

I saw her eyes fill with tears; she laid her hand on mine and said, "Klopstock!" I recalled at once the magnificent ode[3] she had in mind and sank into the stream of emotions which she poured out over me with this password. I could not bear it, bent down over her hand and kissed it amid tears of deepest rapture. And I looked into her eyes again. —Noble man! If you had seen your apotheosis in those eyes! And may I never again hear your name, which has so often been desecrated, from the lips of anyone else!

June 19

I can no longer remember when I left off in my recent story; this much I know: it was two o'clock in the morning when I got to bed, and if I could have talked your ear off instead of writing, I would probably have kept you up till dawn.

I haven't told you yet what happened on our trip home from the dance, and I have no time for doing so today.

It was a most glorious sunrise. The dripping forest, and the refreshed fields all around! The other ladies were falling asleep. She asked me if I didn't want to join the company. I needn't be concerned on her account. "As long as I see those eyes open," I said, looking steadily at her, "there is no danger." —And we held out, both of us, right to her gate, which the maid quietly opened for her, assuring her, in answer to her questions, that her father and the little ones were well and that they were all still asleep. I left her, asking permission to see her again that same day; she granted it and I came; and since that time sun, moon, and stars may calmly carry on their commerce, I don't know whether it is day or night, and the whole world around me is ceasing to exist.

June 21

I spend days as happy as those which God reserves for His saints; and whatever may happen to me in future, I cannot say that I have not experienced the joys, the purest joys, of life. —You know my Wahlheim; I am completely settled in it; from there it is only half an hour's walk to Lotte; there I feel that I am myself, and taste all the happiness that is given to man.

3. *Ode*, allusion to *Die Frühlingsfeir* (1759) by Friedrich Gottlieb Klopstock (1724–1803). Klopstock was the herald of the *Sturm und Drang* through his epic poem *Der Messias* and his odes, which vibrated with passion and were couched in free rhythms. The ode alluded to here was occasioned by a thunderstorm and records the protagonist's emotional response to the storm.

Could I have known, when I chose Wahlheim as the goal of my walks, that it was situated so close to Heaven? How often, on my lengthy walks have I seen, from the mountain or the plain across the river, the hunting lodge which contains all my desires.

My dear Wilhelm, I have made all sorts of reflections about man's desire to extend himself, to make new discoveries, to wander far afield; and then again about his inner impulse to accept limitation willingly, to coast along in the groove of habit and look neither right nor left.

It is wonderful, when I came here and looked down from the hill on the lovely valley, how I was attracted by the prospect about me. —There was the grove! Oh, if only you could mingle with its shade! —Over there was the mountain top. —Oh, if only you could survey the broad expanse from that spot! The chain of hills and the intimate valleys. —Oh, if only I could lose myself in them! —I hurried to the spot and I returned and had not found what I hoped for. Oh, distance is like the future: a great, dim totality lies before the mind, our feelings are submerged in it like our vision, and we yearn, alas, to surrender our whole being, to let ourselves be filled with all the bliss of a single, great, glorious emotion. —But alas! When we hasten to the goal, when There becomes Here, everything is as it was, and we stand there in our poverty, in our narrowness, and our soul pines for the refreshing draught that has eluded it.

So the most restless vagabond finally longs to return to his native land and finds in his little cottage, at the breast of his wife, in the circle of his children, in the labor of supporting them, the bliss he sought in vain in the great world.

When I go out to my Wahlheim at sunrise and there pick my own sugar peas in the garden of the inn, sit down to shell them while I read my Homer; when I then select a pot in the little kitchen, dig out a piece of butter, put the peas on the fire, cover them and sit down nearby to stir them occasionally—then I feel vividly how the arrogant suitors of Penelope slaughtered oxen and swine, cut them up and roasted them.[4] Nothing fills me with such quiet, genuine emotion as the traits of patriarchal life which, thank Heaven, I can weave into my existence without affectation.

How happy I am that I can feel in my heart the simple, innocent joy of the man who brings to his table a head of cabbage which he has grown himself and who now enjoys not only the cabbage, but all the good days, the beautiful morning on which he

4. Penelope, allusion to Homer's *Odyssey*, Book XX, line 251.

planted it, the lovely evenings when he watered it and found pleasure in seeing it grow—steadily enjoying it all once more in that
one moment.

June 29

The day before yesterday the physician came out here from town
to see the magistrate and found me sitting on the floor among
Lotte's children, some of them crawling over me, others teasing me,
and I was tickling them and raising a great uproar with them. The
doctor, who is an extremely dogmatic puppet, who folds his cuffs
and tugs incessantly at his frills as he talks, found this to be
beneath the dignity of an intelligent man; I could see it from the
angle of his nose. But I did not let him disturb me in the least, and
allowed him to continue his very rational discourse while I rebuilt
the children's card houses, which they had demolished. Afterwards
he went about town complaining that the magistrate's children
were spoiled enough, but now Werther was completely ruining
them.

Yes, my dear Wilhelm, children are closer to my heart than
anything else on earth. When I watch them and see in these tiny
creatures the germ of all virtues and all the powers which they will
one day so sorely need; when I glimpse in their obstinacy a future
steadfastness and firmness of character, in their mischievousness
good humor and the facility to slide over the dangers of the world,
and all that so unspoiled, so whole!—always, always at such times
I repeat the golden words of the Teacher of men: "Except ye
become as one of these!"[5] And yet, my dear friend, they who are
our equals, whom we should regard as our models, we treat as infe-
riors. They are supposed to have no will. —But have we none ourselves? In what way are we superior? —Because we are older and
more sensible! —Good Lord in Heaven, You see old children and
young children and nothing else; and Your Son told us long ago
which of the two give You greater joy. But they do not believe in
Him and do not hear Him—that too is an old story, and they mold
their children in their own image and—good-by, Wilhelm, I don't
wish to ramble on any more.

July 1

What Lotte must mean to a sick man I feel in my own poor
heart, which is worse off than that of many a man who languishes
on his sickbed. She will spend a few days in town at the bedside of
some good woman who, in the view of the doctors, is approaching

5. Matthew 18:3.

her end and wishes to have Lotte beside her in her last moments. I went with her last week to visit the pastor of St. ——, a village situated in the mountains about an hour's walk away. We got there at about four o'clock. Lotte had taken her second sister along. When we entered the courtyard of the parsonage, shaded by two tall nut trees, the good old man was sitting on a bench before the front door, and when he saw Lotte, he seemed to revive, forgot his knotted stick and risked walking over to meet her. She ran to him, urged him to sit down and, taking her place beside him, brought many greetings from her father; she embraced his youngest boy, ugly and dirty but the darling of his old age. You should have seen her keeping the old man occupied, raising her voice so that she might be audible to his half-deaf ears, telling him stories about robust young people who had died unexpectedly, about the excellence of Karlsbad,[6] praising his decision to go there next summer, and how she thought he looked much better and was much more cheerful than when she had last seen him. Meanwhile, I had paid my respects to the pastor's wife. The old man became quite cheerful and, as I could not help praising the beautiful nut trees, which were casting such a pleasant shade over us, he began to tell us their history, though with some difficulty. —"That old one," he said, "we don't know who planted that; some say this pastor, some say another. But the younger one back there is as old as my wife, fifty years in October. Her father planted it on the morning of the day on which she was born in the evening. He was my predecessor in office, and I can't tell you how precious the tree was to him; and it is certainly no less so to me. My wife was sitting under it on a log, knitting, when I first came into this courtyard as a poor student twenty-seven years ago." —Lotte asked about his daughter and learned that she had gone out with Herr Schmidt to the meadow where the workers were; the old man continued his story and told how both his predecessor and his daughter had come to like him, and how he had become first his curate and then his successor. Soon after he had finished the story the pastor's daughter came through the garden with the said Herr Schmidt; she welcomed Lotte cordially and I must say I liked her more than a little: a lively, well-formed brunette, who would have been good company for a short stay in the country. Her suitor (for Herr Schmidt at once presented himself in this role) was a gentle, quiet person, who did not wish to join our conversation, although Lotte kept drawing him into it. What distressed me most was the fact that I seemed to notice in his features that it was obstinacy and ill-humor

---

6. Karlsbad in Bohemia (now Czechoslovakia), a famous medicinal bathing resort.

rather than limited intelligence which prevented him from speaking. Unfortunately this soon became only too plain, for during our walk, when Friederike walked with Lotte and occasionally with me too, the gentleman's face, which was brownish in color even normally, darkened so visibly that it was necessary for Lotte to tug at my sleeve and explain to me that I had been too attentive to Friederike. Now there is nothing that annoys me more than when people torment each other, most of all when young people in the flower of life, when they could be most responsive to all the joys of life, spoil those few good days with nonsensical bickering and realize only too late that what they have squandered is irretrievable. This galled me, and toward evening when we returned to the parsonage and were sitting round a table over our sour milk, and the conversation turned to the joys and sorrows of the world, I could not help picking up the thread and making a heartfelt speech against ill-humor. "We human beings," I began, "often complain that there are so few good days and so many bad ones, but it seems to me we are mostly unjustified in complaining. If our hearts were always disposed to enjoy the good that God prepares for us every day, we would also have enough strength to endure evil when it comes." —"But we cannot control our feelings," the parson's wife replied, "how much depends on our constitution! When one doesn't feel well, everything goes wrong." —I conceded this. —"So let's look upon it as a disease," I continued, "and ask if there is no remedy for it." —"That sounds like a good idea," said Lotte, "at least, I believe much depends on ourselves. I know it from my own experience. When something annoys me and makes me peevish, I jump up, walk up and down the garden, singing a few country dance tunes, and in next to no time it's gone." —"That's exactly what I wanted to say," I continued, "ill-humor is just like indolence, for it is a kind of indolence. We are naturally prone to it, and yet if we once have the strength to pull ourselves together, we do our tasks quickly and we find true pleasure in our activity." —Friederike was very attentive and the young man objected that we are not masters of ourselves and have command least of all over our emotions. "We are dealing here," I replied, "with an unpleasant emotion, which everyone, after all, wants to get rid of, but no one knows how far his powers extend until he has tried them. Certainly, anyone who is sick will consult all the doctors and he will not reject the most demanding deprivations nor the bitterest medicines to recover his desired health."—I noticed that the good old man was straining to hear, so that he might take part in our conversation. I turned toward him and raised my voice. "We preach against so many vices," I said, "but I've never yet heard of an attack on ill-humor from the pulpit.[7]—"The city parsons would have to do that," he said, "peasants are never ill-humored. However, it wouldn't hurt occasionally; it would at least be a lesson for my wife and the magistrate." The company laughed and he laughed heartily with us, till he fell into a fit of coughing, which interrupted our conversation for a while; then the young man resumed: "You called ill-humor a vice; it seems to me that's an exaggeration." —"Not at all," I replied, "if what causes harm to ourselves and our neighbor deserves that name. Isn't it enough that we can't make each other happy? Must we also rob each other of the pleasure in which every heart can still indulge itself at times? And name me a man who is ill-humored but is decent enough to conceal it, to bear it alone, without disturbing the happiness of those around him. Or isn't it rather an inner displeasure at our own unworthiness, a dissatisfaction with ourselves, which is always bound up with hostility that is aroused by foolish vanity? We see happy people who have not been made happy by us and find this intolerable." —Lotte smiled at me when she noticed with what agitation I was speaking, and a tear in Friederike's eye spurred me on to continue. "Woe to those," I said, "who make use of their power over someone else's heart to rob it of the simple joys which grow out of it naturally. All the gifts, all the kindness in the world will not for a moment compensate for the loss of that inner happiness which our tyrant's hostile discontent has turned to bitterness."

At this moment my heart was full; the recollection of so many past events forced itself into my mind and my eyes filled with tears.

"If a man only said to himself every day," I exclaimed, "you can do nothing better for your friends than to leave them their joys and increase their happiness by enjoying it with them. Can you give them one drop of comfort when their minds are tormented by a disturbing passion, shaken by grief?

"And when the last, most harrowing illness befalls the being whom you have undermined in her period of flowering, and she lies there in wretched exhaustion, her unseeing eye turned toward heaven, the sweat of death comes and goes on her pale brow, and you stand at her bedside like a man condemned, with the most profound conviction that all your powers are powerless, and anxiety convulses you, so that you would give anything if you could instill a drop of strength, a spark of courage into the dying creature."

The recollection of such a scene at which I had been present

7. We now have an excellent sermon by Lavater on this theme, among those on the book of Jonah [Goethe's note]. The allusion is to *Predigten über das Buch Jonas* (Sermons on the Book of Jonah) (1773) by Johann Kasper Lavater (1741–1801), theologian and physiognomist, whose work Goethe esteemed highly. The sermon in question is entitled: "Mittel gegen Unzufriedenheit und üble Laune" (Remedies for Discontent and Ill-humor).

struck me with full force as I uttered these words. I put my hand-kerchief to my eyes and left the company; and only Lotte's voice calling to me that we were leaving brought me back to myself. And how she scolded me on the way because I took everything too much to heart and that it would destroy me, and that I should spare myself. —Oh, angel! For your sake I must go on living.

July 6

She is constantly with her dying friend, and she is always the same, always there, always the sweet creature who eases pain and brings happiness wherever her eyes alight. Last night she went for a walk with Marianne and little Malchen; I knew of it and met them and we walked together. After an hour and a half we came back toward the town, to the spring which is so precious to me and is now a thousand times more precious. Lotte sat down on the low wall, and we stood before her. I looked around, ah!, and the time when my heart was so alone came back to my memory. "Beloved spring," I said, "since then I have not rested beside your cool waters; sometimes I did not even glance at you as I hurried past." I looked down and saw little Malchen busily climbing up the steps with a glass of water in her hand. —I looked at Lotte and felt all that she means to me. Meanwhile Malchen arrived with the glass. Marianne wanted to take it from her. "No," the child cried with the sweetest expression on her face, "no, Lotte, you must drink first." The sincerity, the sweetness with which she said this so delighted me that I could express my emotion in no other way than by lifting the child off the ground and giving her a hearty kiss; she began to scream and cry. —"You did a bad thing," said Lotte. —I was astonished. "Come, Malchen," she continued, taking her by the hand and leading her down the steps, "wash it off there with the fresh water—quick, quick, then it won't hurt you." —As I stood there watching how zealously the little girl rubbed her cheeks with her wet little hands, with what faith that the miraculous spring would wash away all contamination and save her from the disgrace of getting an ugly beard; now Lotte said, "That's enough," and the child still kept washing zealously, as if much could do more than little—I tell you, Wilhlem, I have never witnessed a baptismal ceremony with more respect, and when Lotte came up, I would gladly have thrown myself at her feet as before a prophet who has washed away the sins of a nation with holy water.

That evening, in the joy of my heart, I couldn't help relating the incident to a man whom I expected to possess some human feeling because he has intelligence; but what a reception I got from him! He said Lotte had done a very bad thing; children should not be deceived; such things cause an incredible amount of error and superstition against which children should be protected from an early age.[8] —I now remember that the man had had his child baptized a week before, so I let the matter pass and in my heart remained loyal to the truth that we should behave toward children as God behaves toward us, making us happiest when He allows us to stumble about in a pleasant illusion.

July 8

What a child I am! To be so greedy for a look from her! What a child I am!—We had gone to Wahlheim. The ladies drove out in a carriage and during our walks I thought I saw in Lotte's black eyes—forgive me, I'm a fool, you should see those eyes. —Let me be brief (I can't keep my eyes open), the ladies got into the carriage, young W———, Selstadt and Audran and I stood around them. They chatted through the carriage door with the fellows, who were certainly a gay and merry lot. —I sought Lotte's eyes; ah, they were going from one person to the next! But they did not light on me, me, me, who stood there devoted only to her. —My heart said a thousand farewells to her. And she did not see me! The carriage drove off and a tear stood in my eyes. I looked after her, and saw Lotte's bonnet lean out of the carriage door, and she turned around to look—ah, at me? —My dear friend! I am suspended in this uncertainty; that is my consolation: perhaps she turned to look at me. Perhaps! —Good night! Oh, what a child I am!

July 10

You should see what a foolish figure I cut when she is mentioned in company! And especially when I am asked how I like her—like her! I hate the word as I hate death. What kind of person must he be who merely likes Lotte, who is not absorbed by her with all his senses and emotions? Like! Someone asked me the other day how I like Ossian![9]

July 11

Frau M——— is very bad; I pray for her life because I endure with Lotte. I rarely see her at the home of my friend,[1] and today she

---

8. The man represents the prosaic, unimaginative Enlightenment.

9. Ossian, see note 9 on p. 63.

1. The identity of this friend is not established in the novel.

told me of a remarkable incident. —Old M—— is a greedy, nasty skinflint, who has harassed and restricted his wife horribly all her life, but she has always been able to scrape by. A few days ago, when the doctor had given her up, she sent for her husband—Lotte was in the room—and addressed him as follows: "I must confess something to you which might cause confusion and vexation after my death. I have until now kept house in as orderly and economical a way as possible, but you must pardon me for cheating you these thirty years. At the beginning of our marriage you fixed a trifling sum of money for the kitchen and other domestic expenses. When our household and our business grew larger, you could not be persuaded to increase my weekly allowance proportionately; in short, you realize that, at a time when you knew our expenses were greatest, you demanded that I get along with seven gulden[2] a week. So without contradicting you, I took the money and got the supplement every week from the receipts, since no one would suspect your wife of robbing the till. I have squandered nothing and would have confidently gone into eternity without making this confession to you, except that the person who will have to keep house after me would not know how to do it on this sum and you could always insist that your first wife had been able to manage."

I talked with Lotte about the incredible blindness of the human mind; how can a person not suspect that something is wrong when his wife makes out with seven gulden and he sees that the expenditure amounts to about double that sum? But I myself have known people who would have accepted the prophet's everlasting oil jug[3] in their home without astonishment.

July 13

No, I am not deceiving myself. I read in her black eyes genuine interest in me and my destiny. Yes, I feel, and in this I may trust my heart, that she—oh, may I, can I express the heaven that is in these words?—that she loves me!

Loves me! —And how precious I become to myself when I—I suppose I may say it to you, you understand such things—how I worship myself since she loves me!

I wonder whether this is presumption or a true understanding of our relationship? —I don't know the man I could fear as a rival for Lotte's heart. And yet—when she speaks of her fiancé with such warmth, with such love—I feel like a man who is stripped of all his honors and titles, and whose sword is taken from him.

---

2. An old coin worth two marks.   3. I Kings 17: 14–16.

July 16

Oh, how the blood courses through my veins when my finger accidentally touches hers, when our feet meet under the table. I withdraw as if I had touched fire, and a secret force draws me forward again—all my senses begin to reel. —Oh, and her innocence, her naive heart does not feel what a torment these little intimacies are to me. When she puts her hand on mine during a conversation and, impelled by her interest, moves closer to me so that the heavenly breath of her mouth can reach my lips—I think I shall fall to the ground as if struck by lightning. —And Wilhelm, if ever I dare to—this heaven, this trust! —You understand me. No, my heart is not so depraved! Weak, weak enough! —And isn't that depravity?—

She is sacred to me. All desire subsides in her presence. I never know what I feel when I am with her; it is as though my soul were whirling in every nerve. She has a tune which she plays on the piano with the touch of an angel, so simple and so spiritual. It is her favorite song and I am cured of all my anguish, confusion, and despondency when she strikes the first note.

Not a word about the ancient magic power of music appears improbable to me. How the simple song moves me! And how she knows when to play it, often when I would like to put a bullet through my head. The confusion and darkness in my mind are dispersed and I breathe more freely again.

July 18

Wilhelm, what is the world to our hearts without love? A magic lantern[4] without light. But as soon as you put the little lamp inside, the most colorful pictures shine on your white screen. And even if it were no more than that, no more than fleeting phantoms, it always makes us happy to stand before them like naïve boys and delight in these marvelous sights. Today I was unable to go to Lotte. Company which I could not avoid detained me. What was I to do? I sent my servant to her, just to have someone about me who had been close to her today. How impatiently I waited for him, and with what joy I welcome him back! I would have liked to take his head and kiss him if I hadn't been ashamed to do so.

They say of Bologna stone that, when placed in the sun, it

---

4. The magic lantern and the peep show (*Raritätenkasten*—See note 5 on p. 49) are favorite images of the early Goethe.

attracts the rays and shines for a time at night. That's the way I felt about the servant. The feeling that her eyes had rested on his face, his cheeks, the buttons of his jacket, and the collar of his overcoat made all these so sacred, so precious to me! At that moment I wouldn't have parted with the boy for a thousand thalers.[5] I felt so happy in his presence. —Heaven help you if you laugh at me. Wilhelm, is it a delusion when we feel happy?

July 19

"I shall see her!" I exclaim in the morning when I'm fully awake and look happily at the beautiful sun, "I shall see her!" And I have no other wish all day. Everything, everything is swallowed up by this prospect.

July 20

I cannot yet accept your suggestion that I should go with the ambassador to ——. I don't like to be a subordinate, and we all know that the man is disagreeable too. You say my mother would like to see me active; that makes me laugh. Am I not active now? And does it make any real difference whether I count peas or lentils? After all, everything in the world ends in the same triviality, and a person who works himself to the bone for others, to gain money or honor or anything else without a passion or need for doing so, is always a fool.

July 24

Since you are so concerned that I should not neglect my drawing, I would rather forget the whole matter than tell you that, for the present, little is being accomplished.

I've never been happier, my feeling for nature, down to a little stone, to a blade of grass, has never been fuller and deeper, and yet—I don't know how to express myself, my imaginative power is so weak, everything swims and quivers before my mind in such a way that I cannot capture a clear outline; but I tell myself: if I had clay or wax I would give it proper form. If this lasts any longer I will actually take clay and knead it, even if I produce nothing but cakes.

I've begun Lotte's portrait three times, and three times I've ruined it, which is all the more annoying because a while ago I was

5. The *thaler* is an old coin worth three marks.

able to do very good likenesses. I have since made her silhouette, and this will have to do.

July 26

Yes, dear Lotte, I will attend to and order everything; just give me more commissions to carry out, and very often. But one thing I beg of you: no more sand[6] on the little notes you write me. Today I swiftly raised your letter to my lips and the sand gritted on my teeth.

July 26

More than once I have made the resolve not to see her so often. If one could only keep such a resolution! Every day I succumb to temptation and make a sacred promise to myself: tomorrow you will just stay away; and when tomorrow comes I find another irresistible reason for going, and before I realize it I'm with her. Either she said the evening before: "You will come tomorrow, won't you?"—who could stay away after that?—or she gives me an errand to do and I find it appropriate to bring her the answer myself, or the day is altogether too beautiful, so I walk to Wahlheim and when I have got that far, it's only another half hour to her! I am too near her atmosphere—zoom, I'm there. My grandmother used to tell a tale about the magnetic mountain. Ships that came too close to it suddenly lost all their iron; the nails flew to the mountain and the poor wretched crew perished amid the collapsing planks.

July 30

Albert has arrived and I shall go. Even if he were the best, the noblest man, whom I could accept as my superior in every respect, it would be intolerable to see him before me in possession of so many perfections. —Possession! —Enough, Wilhelm, the fiancé is here. A nice, dear man, whom one cannot help liking. Fortunately, I was not present when they met. That would have rent my heart. And he's so honorable and hasn't kissed Lotte in my presence a single time. May Heaven reward him for it. I must love him because of the respect he feels for the girl. He's friendly toward me, and I suspect that this is Lotte's work rather than his own sentiment; for women are subtle in these matters, and rightly so; if they can keep two admirers on good terms with each other, the advantage is always on their side, though it rarely works out.

However, I can't deny Albert my esteem. His calm exterior con-

6. Used for blotting.

trasts sharply with the restlessness of my character, which I cannot conceal. He is a man of deep feeling and knows what a treasure he has in Lotte. He seems to have little ill-humor, and you know that is the sin[7] I hate in people more than any other.

He regards me as a man of sensibility;[8] my attachment to Lotte, the warm joy I feel in all her actions increases his triumph, and he loves her all the more for it. I shall not inquire whether he torments her occasionally with petty jealousies, but if I were in his place, I would not be altogether safe from this devil.

Be that as it may, my joy in being with Lotte is gone. Call it foolishness or delusion—what need is there to find a name for it? The thing speaks for itself. —I knew all I know now before Albert came; I knew that I could make no claims on her, and made none— that is, insofar as it is possible not to feel desire in the presence of so much charm—and now the fool stares in astonishment when the other man really appears and takes the girl away from him.

I gnash my teeth and mock at my misery and would be doubly and triply scornful of those who would say I ought to resign myself, because it simply couldn't be any different. —Get these scarecrows off my back! —I ramble in the woods and when I return to Lotte and find Albert sitting beside her in the little garden under the arbor and I can bear it no longer, I am riotously foolish and do absurd and confused things. —"For Heaven's sake," Lotte said to me today, "I beg of you, not another scene like the one last night. You frighten me when you are so merry." —Between you and me, I wait for the time when he's busy elsewhere; zoom! I'm out there, and I'm always happy when I find her alone.

August 8

Please, dear Wilhelm, I certainly didn't mean you when I branded as unbearable those people who demand submission to inevitable destiny. I didn't really believe you would share this opinion. Basically, you're right. But just remember this, my dear fellow: in this world it is rarely an either-or decision; feelings and actions take on as many different shadings as there are gradations between a hawk and a pug nose.

So you will not take it amiss if I grant you your whole argument and yet try to thread my way through the either-or.

---

7. One would expect "vice," as on page 23, line 10. But there, too, the vice was discussed in a theological context.

8. The German text reads: "Er hält mich für einen Mann von Sinn." The Oxford English Dictionary defines *sensibility* as "capacity for refined emotion; delicate sensitiveness of taste."

Either, you say, you have hopes of winning Lotte or you have none. Good, in the first case try to realize them, try to encompass the fulfillment of your wishes; in the other case show yourself to be a man and try to rid yourself of a wretched emotion which is bound to consume all your energies. —My dear fellow, that is well put and—easily said.

But can you demand of the unhappy man, whose life is gradually, inevitably withering away from a lingering disease, can you demand of him that he should bring an abrupt end to his torture with the thrust of a dagger? Does not the disorder which is consuming his energies at the same time rob him of the courage to free himself?

True, you could reply to me with a similar analogy: who would not rather lose an arm than risk his life by hesitating and wavering? —I don't know! —Let us not bite each other with similes. Enough—yes, Wilhelm, at times I experience moments of courage when I jump up and shake it off, and then—I would gladly go away, if I only knew where.

The Same Evening

My diary, which I have neglected for some time, fell into my hands again today, and I am astonished to note how deliberately I have walked into the whole situation step by step. How clearly I have always seen my condition, and yet I have acted like a child; even now I see it very clearly and yet there is no sign of a turn for the better.

August 10

I could lead the best and happiest life here if I weren't a fool. It is not often that one finds such a beautiful conjunction of circumstances designed to delight the heart as that in which I find myself now. Oh, how certain it is that our heart alone makes us happy. —To be a member of this charming family, loved by the old man like a son, like a father by the children, and by Lotte! —And then upright Albert, who does not disturb my happiness by any rude capriciousness, who receives me with cordial friendship, for whom I am, after Lotte, the person he holds dearest in this world! —Wilhelm, it is a joy to hear us when we go for a walk and talk about Lotte; there is nothing in the world more absurd than this relationship, and yet it often brings tears to my eyes.

When he tells me about her fine mother; how, on her deathbed, she turned over her house and her children to Lotte, how she commended Lotte to his care, how Lotte has been inspired by a wholly different spirit since that time, how care for the household and the seriousness of the situation have made a true mother of her, how not a moment of her time has passed without active love or work and yet her cheerfulness, her gaiety have never left her. —I walk along beside him, picking flowers by the roadside; I weave them very carefully into a bouquet—and throw them into the stream that flows past us, looking after them as they float gently with the current. —I don't know whether I've written you that Albert is going to stay here and will be given an office and a handsome salary by the Court, where he is very well liked. I have met few people who are his equals in the orderly and diligent conduct of affairs.

August 12

Certainly, Albert is the best person beneath heaven. I had an extraordinary scene with him yesterday. I went to take leave of him, for I had a sudden wish to ride into the mountains, from where I am writing now; as I was walking up and down the room, his pistols caught my eye. —"Lend me your pistols for my trip," I said. "All right," he replied, "if you want to go to the trouble of loading them; they merely hang in my room *pro forma*." —I took one down and he continued: "Ever since my caution played me a mean trick, I don't want to have anything more to do with the stuff." I was curious to hear the story. "I was staying," he related, "at the house of a friend in the country for some three months. I had a pair of unloaded pistols and slept in peace. Once on a rainy afternoon I was sitting there doing nothing, I don't know what gave me the idea that we might be attacked and might need the pistols, and—you know how those things are. —I gave them to my servant to clean and load. He was dallying with the maids, trying to frighten them, when, Heaven knows how it happened, the weapon went off and, since the ramrod was still in the barrel, it went right through the ball of one girl's thumb, smashing it. I had to stand all her wailing and pay the costs of her cure as well, and since that time I have left all my weapons unloaded. My dear fellow! What use is caution? You can never anticipate every danger. Of course——" Now, you know, I like the man very much except for his "of courses"; for is it not obvious that every general statement has its exceptions? But the man is so anxious to be exactly right, that if he thinks he has said something overhasty, too general, or half-true, he won't stop limiting, modifying, adding, and subtracting, until finally there is nothing left of the statement. And on this occasion he got very deeply into his subject; at last I stopped listening to him altogether, fell into a despondent mood and, with a vehement gesture, I pressed the mouth of the pistol to my forehead above my right eye. "Shame!" Albert said, pulling the pistol away from me. "What's the meaning of this?" "But it isn't loaded," I said. —"Even so, what's the meaning of it?" he repeated impatiently. "I can't imagine anyone being foolish enough to shoot himself; the mere thought of it repels me."

"Why must you people," I exclaimed, "when you speak about anything, say at once, this is foolish, this is wise, this is good, this is bad? And what does all this mean? Have you investigated the hidden circumstances behind an action? Can you reveal with certainty the reasons why it happened, why it had to happen? If you had done so, you wouldn't be so hasty with your judgments."

"You will admit," said Albert, "that certain actions remain vicious, no matter what the motive for them may be."

I shrugged my shoulders and admitted it. "But, my friend," I continued, "there are some exceptions here too. It is true that theft is a crime; but does the man who commits a robbery to save himself and his family from imminent starvation deserve sympathy or punishment? Who will lift the first stone against the husband who, in righteous anger, sacrifices his unfaithful wife and her unworthy seducer? against the girl who, in an hour of bliss, succumbs to the irresistible joys of love? Even our laws, those cold-blooded pedants, permit themselves sympathy and withhold their punishment."

"That's quite a different matter," Albert replied, "because a person who is carried away by his passions loses all power of judgment and is viewed as a drunkard or madman."

"Oh you sensible people!" I exclaimed with a smile. "Passion! Drunkenness! Madness! You stand there so calm, so unsympathetic, you moral people. You condemn the drunkard, abhor the man bereft of his reason, pass by like the priest and thank God like the Pharisee that He did not make you as one of these.[9] I have been drunk more than once, my passions have never been far from madness, and I regret neither; for, at my own level, I have come to appreciate why all extraordinary people who have achieved something great, something apparently impossible, have been inevitably decried by society as drunkards or madmen.

"But even in everyday life, whenever someone does something that is halfway free, noble, unexpected, it is intolerable to hear them cry: the man is drunk, he's mad! Shame on you, you sober people! Shame on you, wise men!"

9. Priest, Luke 10:31; Pharisee, Luke 18:11.

"These are more of your queer notions," Albert said. "You exaggerate everything, and in this instance at least you are certainly wrong in comparing suicide, which is the subject under discussion, with great deeds, since it cannot be regarded as anything but a weakness. For, to be sure, it is certainly easier to die than to endure a life of torment with fortitude."

I was on the point of breaking off, for no argument so disconcerts me as when someone drags in some insignificant platitude when I am talking from the depths of my heart. But I controlled myself because I had heard the argument often before and had been annoyed by it frequently; and I replied with some spirit: "You call that weakness? I beg of you, don't be misled by appearances. When a nation has long groaned under the intolerable yoke of a tyrant and finally rises up and breaks its chains, you dare call it weak? A man who feels all his energies redoubled by the terror of seeing his house in flames, and easily carries away burdens which he can scarcely move when his mind is calm; someone who, in the fury of an insult, takes on six people and overpowers them—can these be called weak? And, my good friend, if effort is strength, why should supreme effort be the opposite?" —Albert looked at me and said: "Excuse me for saying so, but the examples you have given don't seem to apply to the situation at all." —"That may be," I said, "I have often heard the reproach that my logic at times borders on absurdity. So let us see if we can somehow imagine how a person may feel when he decides to throw off the normally pleasant burden of life. For only to the extent that we can put ourselves in another man's situation are we justified in talking about a matter.

"Human nature," I continued, "has its limits. It can endure joy, sorrow, and pain up to a certain point and goes to pieces as soon as this point is passed. The question, therefore, is not whether a man is weak or strong, but whether he can endure the measure of his suffering, be it mental or physical. And I find it just as strange to say that the man who takes his own life is a coward, as it would be improper to call the man who dies of a malignant fever a coward."

"Paradoxical! Very paradoxical!" Albert exclaimed. —"Not as much as you think," I replied. "You will admit that we speak of a sickness unto death,[1] by which the system is so deeply affected that its energies are partly exhausted, partly put out of commission, so that they are not capable of recovering, of restoring the normal course of life, through some fortunate turn of events.

1. Sickness unto death: John 11:4; later used by Kierkegaard as the title of a book which refutes Werther's thesis.

"Now, my good friend, let us apply this to the mind. Look at man with all his limitations, how he is affected by impressions, how ideas take root in him, until finally a growing passion robs him of his powers of calm reflection and destroys him.

"It is in vain that a relaxed, rational person grasps the unhappy man's condition, in vain does he attempt to talk to him persuasively. Just as a healthy man standing at the bedside of a sick person cannot transfer to him even the slightest quantity of his own strength."

This talk was too general for Albert. I reminded him of a girl who had recently been found dead in the water and repeated her story to him. "A decent young creature who had grown up in the narrow sphere of domestic duties, of a weekly schedule of tasks that included no prospect of amusement, except perhaps to stroll about town on Sunday with girls of similar station, dressed in the finery she had gradually accumulated; perhaps to go to a dance on the principal holidays, and for the rest to spend the odd hour gossiping with a neighbor, in complete emotional involvement, about the cause of a quarrel or an item of scandal. —Finally, her warm nature experiences deeper needs which are nourished by the flattery of men; her former sources of gratification lose their savor bit by bit, until she finally meets a man to whom she is irresistibly drawn by a hitherto unknown feeling, on whom she now pins all her hopes, forgetting the world about her, hearing nothing, seeing nothing, feeling nothing but him, the only one; longing only for him, for him alone. Uncorrupted by the empty pleasures of fickle vanity, her desire moves straight toward its goal; she wants to become his; she wants to find in an eternal union all the happiness she lacks, to enjoy the sum of all the bliss for which she yearned. Repeated promises which put the seal of certainty on all her hopes, bold caresses which increase her desire, possess the whole being; she floats in a state of vague consciousness, in an anticipation of complete bliss, she has attained a state of highest tension. At last she stretches out her arms to embrace all her wishes—and her lover abandons her. —Stunned, her senses numbed, she stands before an abyss; all around her is darkness, no prospect, no consolation, no vision of a way out! The man in whom alone she felt her existence has forsaken her. She does not see the great world that lies before her, nor the many others who could compensate her for her loss; she feels herself alone, forsaken by the whole world—and blindly, driven into a corner by the dreadful anguish of her heart, she plunges into the depths to stifle all her torment in an all-encompassing death.[2] —See, Albert, that is the story of many, many

1a. This account is based on an actual suicide in Frankfurt am Main that occurred in 1769. Anna Elisabeth Stöber, daughter of a cabinet maker, drowned herself in the river Main under circumstances which approximate to Goethe's description here.

people! Tell me, isn't that a case of sickness? Nature finds no way out of the labyrinth of confused and contradictory forces, so man must die.

"I feel sorry for the man who could look on this and say: 'The foolish girl! If she had waited, if she had allowed time to work its effect, her despair would have subsided, another man would have come forward to console her.' —That's just as if one were to say: 'What a fool, to die of a fever! If he had waited till his strength had restored itself, his humors[2] improved, the tumult of his blood calmed down, all would have been well and he would be alive this very day!'"

Albert, to whom the analogy was not yet clear, made some other objections, including the one that my story concerned a simple-minded girl; but how one could excuse an intelligent person who was not so limited and had a broader grasp of things, was beyond his comprehenison. —"My friend," I exclaimed, "man is man and the modicum of intelligence that we may possess is of small or no account when passion rages and we are constrained by the limits of our human condition. Rather—but let's talk of this some other time," I said, snatching up my hat. Oh, my heart was so full! —And we parted, without having understood each other. As, indeed, no one easily understands another in this world.

August 15

One thing is certain: nothing in the world makes a person indispensable except love. I feel that Lotte would be sorry to lose me, and the children simply assume that I will come again the next day. I had gone out today to tune Lotte's piano, but I couldn't get to the job because the children hounded me to tell them a fairy tale, and Lotte herself asked me to grant them their wish. I cut the bread for their supper, a service they now accept almost as willingly from me as from Lotte, and told them the favorite story of the princess who is served by hands. I assure you that I learn a lot from this storytelling and I'm astonished at the deep impression my stories make on them. Sometimes I must invent a minor episode, which I forget when I repeat the tale; at once they tell me that it was different last time, so that I now practice reciting the story in a singsong tone, like clockwork. From this I've learned that an author must inevitably hurt his book by issuing a second, revised edition of his story, no matter how greatly it may be improved from the liter-

2. The juices in the body which, according to the old physiology, regulate the proper functioning of the system.

ary point of view. The first impression finds us receptive, and man is so constituted that he can be persuaded to believe the strangest things; but these impressions at once cling firmly to his memory, and woe to him who tries to erase and destroy them.

August 18

Did it have to be so, that what makes a man happy should also become the source of his misery?

The full, warm feeling in my heart for living nature which flooded me with so much joy, which transformed the world about me into a paradise, is now becoming a source of unbearable torment for me, a torturing demon which pursues me everywhere. When I used to survey the fertile valley from this rock and gaze cross the river to those hills beyond, and see everything around me budding and swelling; when I saw the mountains, clad from foot to summit in tall, dense trees, and saw the meandering valleys shaded by the loveliest forests, with the gentle stream gliding along among the whispering reeds, mirroring the lovely clouds which the gentle evening breeze wafted across the sky; when I then heard the birds about me enliven the woods and saw the millions of insects dancing gaily in the last red radiance of the setting sun, whose last quivering glance freed the humming beetle from the grass, and the buzzing and stirring about me made me conscious of the ground and the moss which wrests its nourishment from my hard rock, and the shrubbery which grows down the arid sand hill opened up to me the inner, glowing, sacred life of nature—how I gathered all this into my warm heart, felt myself like a god in my overflowing abundance, and the glorious forms of the infinite world stirred in my soul, giving life to everything. Enormous mountains surrounded me, abysses lay before me, and cataracts rushed down; the rivers flowed by below me, and the forests and mountains resounded from the echo; and I saw them, all those unfathomable forces, creatively at work[3] on each other in the depths of the earth; and now above the earth and beneath the sky the myriad races of creatures swarm. Everything, everything populated by a thousand forms, and the humans then seek security close together in little houses, put down roots and rule the great world in their own way! Poor fool, in whose opinion everything is so insignificant because you are so small! —From the inaccessible mountain range to the wasteland which no foot has ever trod, and on to the end of the unexplored

---

3. The German text has *wirken* (produce), for Herder and the youthful Goethe equivalent to *schaffen* (create), emphasizing the idea of *natura naturans* (dynamic, restlessly productive nature).

ocean, the spirit of the Eternal Creator stirs, rejoicing in every speck of dust which perceives Him and lives. —Oh, how often did I then yearn to take the wings of a crane which flew overhead, and make for the shore of the boundless sea, to drink from the foaming cup of infinity that effervescent rapture of life, and to feel for only one moment, in my limited mental powers, a drop of the bliss of that Being Who creates all things in and through Himself.

Brother, the mere recollection of those hours does me good. Even the effort to recall these inexpressible feelings, to express them again, lifts my soul above itself, but also makes me feel doubly the wretchedness of the condition that surrounds me now.

A curtain has been drawn before my soul, so to speak, and the stage of infinite life is being transformed before my eyes into the abyss of an ever-open grave. Can you say "this is," when everything is transitory, when everything rolls by with the speed of a tempest and seldom lasts until its whole force is spent, but is swept along, alas, engulfed by the current and shattered on the rocks? There is not a moment that does not consume you and those close to you, not a moment in which you are not a destroyer, and necessarily so; the most innocent stroll costs the lives of a thousand poor little worms; one step destroys the laborious structures erected by the ants and tramples a small world into a miserable grave. Ha! it is not the rare, great misfortunes in the world that move me, not the floods that wash away your villages, nor the earthquakes that engulf your cities; my heart is undermined by the destructive power that lies hidden in the universe of nature, which has created nothing that has not destroyed its neighbor, even itself. And so I stumble about in anguish, with heaven and earth and all the active forces around me; I see nothing but a monster that perpetually devours, eternally ruminates.

August 21

In vain I stretch out my arms toward her in the morning, when I wake from heavy dreams, in vain I seek her at night in my bed when a happy, innocent dream has deceived me into thinking that I was sitting beside her on the meadow, holding her hand and covering it with a thousand kisses. Oh, when I then grope for her, still half drunk with sleep, and then become fully awake through this act—a stream of tears breaks from my anguished heart, and I weep at the hopelessness of a dark future.

August 22

It is a catastrophe, Wilhelm, my active powers have atrophied into an uneasy indolence; I can't be idle and yet I can do nothing.

I have no power of imagination, no feeling for nature, and books disgust me.[4] When we feel inadequate to ourselves, everything seems inadequate to us.[5] I swear to you, I sometimes wish I were a day laborer, if only on awakening in the morning to have a prospect for the coming day, a motive, a hope. I often envy Albert, whom I see up to his ears in documents, and I imagine I would feel happy if I were in his place. Several times already the idea suddenly came to me to write you and the minister, to apply for the embassy post which you assure me would not be refused me. I think you are right. The minister has liked me a long time and has long urged me to embrace some profession; and for an hour I take the idea seriously. Then when I think of it again, and I recall the fable of the horse which, weary of its freedom, allowed itself to be saddled and bridled and was ridden to death[6]—I don't know what I should do. —And, my dear friend, is my longing for a change of condition perhaps only an irritating inner impatience which will pursue me everywhere?

August 28[7]

In truth, if my illness could be cured, these people would cure it. Today is my birthday, and early in the morning I received a little package from Albert. Upon opening it, I noticed at once one of the pink ribbons that Lotte was wearing on her dress front when I was introduced to her and for which I have asked her several times since. There were two little volumes in *duodecimo*,[8] the little Wetstein Homer, an edition I have long craved, so that I would not have to drag the Ernesti edition about with me on my walks. You see how they anticipate my wishes, how they hunt out all the little favors of friendship which are worth a thousand times more than those splendid gifts which humiliate us because they betray the vanity of the donor. I kiss this ribbon a thousand times, and with every breath I drink in the memory of those raptures which filled me during those few, happy, irrevocable days. Wilhelm, it is so, and I do not complain; the flowers of life are mere phantoms. How

4. Werther's mental condition resembles that of Faust in the opening scene of Goethe's drama. Compare also Mallarmé's poem *Brise marine*, which begins: "La chair est triste, hélas! et j'ai lu tous les livres."

5. This is the leitmotif of much of Thomas Mann's early fiction. Compare the key reflection of his hero in *The Clown*: "For let us be honest about it, it matters what you think of yourself, what you want others to think of you, what you have the confidence to make others think of you." This is a recur-

ring motif in *Werther*.

6. The horse asks man to help him in his battle against the stag, but finds that he loses his freedom as a result of the help offered him.

7. August 28th is Goethe's birthday.

8. *Duodecimo*, small in size (because the sheet is folded twelve times). J. H. Wetstein was the printer of the duodecimo edition, which appeared in Amsterdam in 1707; J. A. Ernesti was the editor of the five-volume quarto (large page) edition, published at Leipzig (1759–1764).

many fade without leaving a trace behind them, how few of them produce fruit, and how few of those fruits ripen! And yet there are enough left; and yet—oh, my brother, can we allow ripened fruit to be neglected, despised, and to rot without being enjoyed?

Farewell! It is a glorious summer; I often sit in the fruit trees in Lotte's orchard with the fruit picker, a long pole, plucking pears from the top of the tree. She stands below and takes them from me as I hand them to her.

August 30

Unhappy man! Aren't you a fool? Aren't you deceiving yourself? What sense is there in this raging, endless passion? I no longer have prayers except to her; no other form appears to my imagination except hers, and I see everything in the world about me only in relation to her. And this brings me many a happy hour—until I must tear myself away from her again. Oh Wilhelm! The things my heart often urges me to do! —When I have been sitting with her for two or three hours and have feasted on her figure, her manner, the divine expression of her thoughts, and then gradually my senses become tense, a darkness appears before my eyes, I can scarcely hear anything, my throat is constricted as though by the hand of an assassin, and my heart beats wildly trying to relieve my oppressed senses, but only increasing their confusion—Wilhelm, often I don't know whether I really exist. And at times—when melancholy does not get the upper hand and Lotte permits me the wretched comfort of shedding my tears of anguish on her hand—I must leave her, I must get outside and roam far through the fields; I then find my pleasure in climbing a steep mountain, cutting a path through an untrodden forest, through hedges which tear me, through thorns which rend me. Then I feel a little better. A little. And sometimes I lie down on the way, overcome by weariness and thirst; sometimes in the depth of night, when the full moon stands high above me in the lonely forest, I sit down on a gnarled, crooked tree, to afford some relief to my aching soles, and then I doze off in the twilight in an exhausted sleep. Oh Wilhelm! The solitary dwelling of a cell, the hair shirt, and belt of thorns are the comforts for which my soul yearns. Good-by; I see no end to this misery but the grave.

September 3

I must leave this place! I thank you, Wilhelm, for strengthening my wavering resolution. For two weeks now I've been nursing the thought of leaving her. I must go. She's in town again visiting a friend. And Albert—and—I must leave!

September 10

What a night that was, Wilhelm! Now I can bear anything. I shall not see her again. Oh, why can't I fly to you, embrace you, and express to you, my dear friend, with a thousand tears and raptures, the emotions that beset my heart. Here I sit gasping for breath, trying to calm myself, waiting for morning to come, and the horses have been ordered for sunrise.

Ah, she is sleeping peacefully and does not suspect that she will never see me again. I've torn myself away, and I was strong enough not to betray my intention in a conversation lasting two hours. And Heaven, what a conversation!

Albert had promised me that he would be in the garden[9] with Lotte right after supper. I was standing on the terrace under the tall chestnut trees, looking at the sun which was now setting for me for the last time over the lovely valley and the gentle stream.[1] I had stood here with her so often and watched this same glorious spectacle, and now—I paced up and down the walk that was so precious to me; a secret sympathy had so often held me here, even before I knew Lotte, and how happy we were to discover, at the beginning of our acquaintance, our mutual affection for this spot, which is truly one of the most romantic that I have ever seen created by art.[2]

First, you have the expansive view between the chestnut trees. —Oh, I remember, I think I've already written you a lot about it, how you are finally closed in by high walls of beeches, and how the walk becomes darker and darker because of an adjacent copse, until you reach a small enclosed square that is surrounded by all the thrills of solitude. I can still remember how mysterious it felt when I stepped into it for the first time at high noon; I had a very faint premonition that this would some day become the setting for bliss and pain.

For about half an hour I had revelled in the sweet, languishing thoughts of departure and return, when I felt a thrill as I heard them coming up the terrace. I ran toward them; I took her hand

9. The Count's garden described on page 2, lines 11 ff.

1. Werther unconsciously assumes proprietorship over nature and the places that attract him. This is not ar-rogance but indicative of a high degree of intimacy or perhaps of a feeling that life for him is now at an end.

2. Although the garden was made by man, it was romantic, i.e., natural.

and kissed it. We had just reached the top when the moon rose behind the wooded hill; we talked about all sorts of things and, without being aware of it, approached the secluded garden house. Lotte went in and sat down, Albert beside her, I too; but my restlessness would not permit me to sit long; I stood up, went up to her, walked back and forth, sat down again; my state was an uneasy one. She called our attention to the beautiful effect of the moonlight, which illuminated the whole terrace lying before us at the end of the wall of beech trees; a magnificent sight which was all the more striking because we were surrounded by a deep twilight. We were silent, and after a while she began: "I never go walking in the moonlight without thinking of my deceased ones; without being overcome by the feeling of death, of life after death. We shall be!" she continued in a voice vibrant with the most glorious emotion. "But, Werther, shall we ever find each other again, and know each other again? What do you believe? What do you say?"

"Lotte,"I said, giving her my hand, and my eyes filled with tears, "we shall see each other again, both here and hereafter!" —I could not go on—Wilhelm, did she have to ask me that, when I had this anguished departure in my heart.

"And I wonder whether the dear departed ones know about us," she continued, "whether they feel, when we are happy, that we remember them with warm love? Oh! the form of my mother always hovers about me when I sit on a quiet evening among her children, among my children, and they are gathered about me as they were gathered about her. Then, when I look up to heaven with tears of longing in my eyes and wish that she might look in for a moment and see how I am keeping the promise I gave her in the hour of her death: that I would be the mother of her children. With what emotion I cry out: 'Forgive me, dearest one, if I am not to them what you were. Oh, I am really doing everything I can; they are dressed, fed, and what is more than all that, cared for and loved. If you could see the harmony between us, dear sainted one! you would glorify with the most ardent gratitude the God to whom you prayed for the welfare of your children with your last, most bitter tears.'"

She said this! Oh Wilhelm, who can repeat all that she said? How can the cold, dead letter convey this heavenly flowering of the spirit? Albert interrupted her gently: "You are too deeply moved, dear Lotte! I know you are strongly attached to these ideas, but I beg you" "Oh, Albert," she said, "I know you haven't forgotten the evenings when we sat together at the little round table when papa was away on a trip and we had sent the children to bed.

You often had a good book, but rarely got the chance to read anything. Wasn't the association with that splendid soul worth more than anything else? That beautiful, gentle, bright, and always busy woman! God knows the tears with which I often threw myself before Him in my bed, praying that He might make me like her."

"Lotte!" I exclaimed, throwing myself at her feet, taking her hand and wetting it with a thousand tears, "Lotte, the blessing of God and the spirit of your mother rest upon you!" "If only you had known her," she said, pressing my hand, "she was worthy of being known by you." I thought I would faint. Never had a greater, prouder word been uttered about me and she continued: "And this woman had to pass away in the flower of her years, when her youngest son was not yet six months old. Her illness did not last long, she was calm, resigned; only the thought of her children, especially the youngest, caused her pain. When her end was approaching and she said to me: 'Bring them up to me,' and when I led them in, the little ones who didn't know what was happening, and the oldest, who were in despair as they stood about the bed; and when she raised her hands and prayed over them, and kissed them one after the other and sent them away and said to me: 'Be a mother to them!' I gave her my hand on it. 'You are promising much, my daughter,' she said, 'a mother's heart and a mother's eyes. I have often seen from your tears of gratitude that you feel what that means. Show it to your brothers and sisters, and for your father have the faithfulness and obedience of a wife. You will bring him consolation.' —She asked for him, he had gone out to conceal from us the unbearable grief he felt; the man was completely broken.

"Albert, you were in the room. She heard someone moving about, asked who it was, and called you to her; and when she looked at you and at me, with that calm look of relief because we would be happy, happy together." —Albert threw his arms about her and kissed her and cried: "We are happy, and we shall be!" —The sedate Albert was completely beside himself and I was on the verge of swooning.

"Werther," she began again, "and this woman had to leave us! Lord! When I sometimes think how we let the most precious thing in our lives be carried away, and no one felt it as keenly as the children, who complained long afterwards that the black men had carried off their mama."

She stood up and I was brought back to myself, shaken; I sat there holding her hand. —"Let us go," she said, "it's time to leave." She wanted to withdraw her hand but I held onto it more tightly. "We'll see each other again," I cried, "we shall find each other, we shall recognize each other among all the forms in the beyond. I'm going," I continued, "I go willingly, and yet if I were to say 'forever' I could not bear it. Farewell, Lotte! Farewell, Albert! We shall meet again." "Tomorrow, I suppose," she replied in a jesting tone. —I was stirred by this "tomorrow." Ah, she did not know, as she withdrew her hand from mine. —They went away along the walk; I stood there looking after them in the moonlight, then flung myself on the ground and wept till I could weep no more, leaped up, and ran out on the terrace from where I could still see her white dress gleaming, as it moved toward the garden gate, down in the shadow of the tall linden trees. I stretched out my arms and it vanished.

Book Two

We arrived here yesterday. The ambassador is indisposed and will, therefore, not be available for a few days. If only he weren't so unpleasant, all would be well. I can see, I can see, destiny has harsh trials in store for me. But courage! A light heart endures anything. A light heart? I have to laugh to see these words come from my pen. Oh, if my blood were a bit lighter, I would be the happiest man under the sun. What! where others, with their little bit of energy and talent, swagger about before me in comfortable self-complacency, am I to despair of my powers, my gifts? Good Lord, who have given me all this, why did You not withhold half of it and give me self-confidence and contentment?

Patience, patience! things will improve. For I tell you, my dear friend, you are right. Since I have been drifting about among these people every day, observing how they live and act, I'm much more satisfied with myself. Of course, since we are so constituted that we compare everything with ourselves and ourselves with everything, happiness or misery lies in the objects of the comparison, and so nothing is more dangerous than solitude. Our power of imagination, compelled by its nature to sublimate itself, nourished by the fantastic images of literature, creates a series of beings of whom we are the lowest, and everything outside ourselves seems more splendid to us, everyone else more perfect than we are. The process is a perfectly natural one. We feel so often that we lack many things, and the very things we lack someone else often seems to possess, and we also attribute to him all that we have ourselves, and a certain ideal[1] contentment into the bargain. And so the happy man stands there in perfection, a creature of our own making.

On the other hand, if we but continue to work ahead, with all our weakness and effort, we very often find that, in spite of our straggling and tacking, we get farther than others with their sailing and rowing—and—it is, after all, a true feeling of satisfaction to keep up with or actually outdistance others.

1. I.e., born in our imagination.

November 26, 1771

I am beginning to find life here quite tolerable, everything considered. The best thing about it is that there is enough to do; and then the many kinds of people, the great variety of new types, present a gay spectacle before my mind's eye. I have become acquainted with Count C——, a man whom I am compelled to respect more and more every day, a man of broad and great understanding, who, though able to comprehend much, is not unsympathetic; my association with him clearly demonstrates his great capacity for friendship and love. He showed an interest in me when I went to him on a matter of business, and he perceived after our first words that we understood each other, that he could talk to me better than to most people. Moreover, I cannot praise his frank behavior toward me highly enough. There is no other joy so true or so warm in this world as that of finding a great soul responding to your own.

December 24, 1771

The ambassador is causing me much annoyance, as I anticipated. He is the most punctilious fool on earth; he does things step by step and is as fussy as an old woman; a man who is never satisfied with himself and whom it is, therefore, impossible to please. I like to work casually and to leave things as they come out; but he's capable of handing a document back to me and saying, "It's good, but look through it again, you can always find a better word, a more appropriate particle." [2] —I could go mad! No "and," no conjunction may be left out, and he's a mortal enemy to every inversion that may occasionally escape me; if you don't pound out your periods according to the traditional melody, he's completely bewildered. It's martyrdom to deal with such a person.

The confidence shown me by Count C—— is the only thing that offers me some compensation. He recently told me quite frankly how dissatisfied he was with the slowness and pedantry of my ambassador. "Such people make things hard for themselves and for others; however," he added, "you must resign yourself to it like a traveler who has to go over a mountain; of course, if the mountain weren't there, the road would be much more convenient and shorter; but there it is, so you must get over it!"—

2. Werther means conjunction, as he explains in the sentence after the next. This stylistic unorthodoxy and the use of inversions (i.e., beginning a sentence with an adverbial or adjectival phrase rather than with the subject) were characteristic of the young *Sturm-und-Drang* rebels. Goethe's early letters are full of them, whereas his legal writings of the same period are entirely free from them.

The old man no doubt senses that the Count prefers my company to his, and this annoys him, and he seizes every opportunity to tell me bad things about the Count; I naturally contradict him and that only makes matters worse. Yesterday he really aroused me, for he included me in his censure: the Count, he said, is quite well-suited for the affairs of the world, he works easily and writes a good style; but, like all men of letters, he lacks thorough scholarship. And in saying this he made a face as if to say: "Do you feel the jab?" But it missed its effect on me; I felt contempt for a man who could think and act in this way. I stood my ground and fought back quite vigorously. I said the Count was a man whom one had to respect both for his character and for his knowledge. "I've never known anyone," I said, "who has been so successful in broadening his mind, extending it over such a vast field and who yet continues to be active in everyday life." —This was all Greek to his puny brain, and I took my leave, so that I would not have to swallow even more anger over his twaddle.

And you are all to blame for this, for you talked me into putting on this yoke and sang me such a song about an active life. An active life! If the man who plants potatoes and rides to town to sell his wheat doesn't do more than I am doing, I will spend ten more years slaving on the galley to which I am now chained.

And the glittering misery, the boredom among these horrid people who gather here! Their snobbery, which keeps them awake and alert to get one tiny step ahead of the others: the most wretched, most pitiable passions, in all their nakedness. There is a woman here, for instance, who never stops talking about her nobility and her country,[3] so that everyone who doesn't know her is forced to think: that woman's a fool, to have such absurd illusions about her scrap of nobility and the renown of her country. —But it's even much worse than that: this same woman is the daughter of a magistrate's clerk from near-by. —Really, I can't understand our human race, that has so little sense to behave with such base stupidity.

Though I must say, my friend, that I notice more and more every day how foolish it is to judge others by oneself. And because I am so preoccupied with myself and my heart is so tempestuous—oh, I'll gladly let the others go their own way if only they will let me go mine.

What provokes me most of all is the disagreeable social conditions in this place. Of course, I know as well as the next man how

---

3. One of the numerous sovereign states (large or small) that made up the Holy Roman Empire of the German Nation.

necessary it is to have class differences, and what advantages I myself derive from them; but I won't have them stand in my way toward experiencing a little joy, a gleam of happiness on this earth. Recently, while I was taking a walk, I became acquainted with a Fräulein von B——, a charming creature, who has remained quite natural in the midst of an artificial existence. We enjoyed our conversation, and when we parted I asked permission to call on her. She gave me leave to do so with such frankness that I could hardly wait for the appropriate moment to go to her home. She is not from this region, and lives with an aunt. I did not like the old lady's physiognomy. I was very attentive to her, my conversation was mostly directed to her, and in less than half an hour I was fairly certain of what the young lady subsequently admitted to me: that her dear aunt has nothing in her old age: no respectable fortune, no intelligence, no support except her pedigree, no security except her social rank, behind which she entrenches herself, and no enjoyment except to look down from her upstairs on the common heads below. She is said to have been beautiful in her youth, and to have frittered away her life, torturing many a poor young man with her caprices, while in her more mature years she submitted obediently to an old officer who, in return for this obedience and tolerable economic support, spent his bronze age[4] with her and then died. Now she finds herself alone in her iron age, and would not even be noticed if her niece were not so charming.

January 8, 1772

What sort of people are they, whose whole mental lives revolve around ceremony, who for years direct all their thoughts and efforts toward the goal of moving one chair higher up at the dinner table! Not that they have nothing better to do; no, on the contrary, the work piles up simply because these petty annoyances keep them from attending to important matters. Last week a quarrel broke out during a sleigh ride and all the fun was spoiled.

Can't the fools see that position doesn't matter at all, and that the man who has first place rarely plays the principal role? How many kings are ruled by their ministers, and how many ministers by their secretaries! And who is first then? The man, it seems to me, who controls others, and possesses enough power or cunning to harness their energies and passions for the execution of his own plans.

---

4. Classical writers divided history into four periods or ages: the golden, silver, bronze, and iron; each age was regarded as being inferior to the preceding one. This scheme is here applied to individual man's existence.

January 20

I must write to you, dear Lotte, here in the main room of a humble country inn, in which I have sought shelter from a severe storm. As long as I moved about in the sad hole D——, among people who were totally alien to my mind, there was not a moment, not a single moment, in which my heart urged me to write to you; but now, in this cabin, in this solitude, in this confinement, when snow and sleet batter my little window, here you were my first thought. As I entered the place, your image, oh Lotte, the memory of you, filled me with such sacred warmth! Kind God, the first happy moment again!

If you could see me, my dear, in this orgy of distraction! How desiccated my senses become; not one moment of plenitude for my heart, not one hour of happiness! Nothing, nothing! I stand as before a peep show[5] and see the tiny men and horses racing around before my eyes, and keep asking myself whether it isn't an optical illusion. I, too, play the game, or rather I am played like a puppet, and sometimes I grasp my neighbor's wooden hand and start back in horror. In the evening I resolve to enjoy the sunrise, but I don't get out of bed; by day I hope to enjoy the moonlight, but I remain in my room. I don't really know why I get up or why I go to bed.

The leaven that used to set my life in motion is lacking; the stimulus which kept me alert in the deep nights and awakened me out of my sleep in the morning is gone.

I have met one sole female being here, a Fräulein von B——; she resembles you, dear Lotte, if anyone can resemble you. "My," you will say, "the man is indulging in pretty compliments." That's not altogether untrue. For some time I've been very gallant, because I can't be anything else; I have much wit, and the ladies say that no one can dispense such elegant praise as I (or lie, you will add, for it can't be done without lying, don't you see?). I was going to talk about Fräulein von B——. She has much refinement, which shines out fully from her blue eyes. Her social position is a burden to her, satisfying none of her heart's desires. She longs to be out of this turmoil, and we dream away many an hour in rustic scenes of unalloyed bliss; ah, and about you! How often does she have to pay homage to you, doesn't have to—but does it willingly; takes such pleasure in hearing about you, loves you.—

Oh, I wish I were sitting at your feet in that dear, familiar little

5. *Raritätenkasten*, a box with a hole in front; peeping through the hole, one sees tiny figures moving about, illustrating some story. These boxes were hawked about at German fairs. This image is a favorite of the young Goethe.

room, with our dear little children tumbling about me, and if they became too noisy for you, I would gather them about me and calm them with an eerie fairy tale.

The sun is setting gloriously over the snow-covered region, the storm has passed, and I—must lock myself in my cage once more. —Adieu! Is Albert with you? And how——? Heaven forgive me this question!

February 8

For a week we have been having the most horrible weather, but it's beneficial for me. For as long as I've been here there hasn't been a single beautiful day which someone has not spoiled or marred for me. Now, when it rains hard and the wind blows and it freezes and thaws—ha! I think, it can't get worse in the house than it is outside or vice versa, and so it's all right. If the sun goes up in the morning and promises a fine day, I never fail to exclaim: there is another gift from Heaven of which they can deprive each other. There is nothing they wouldn't take from each other: health, reputation, joy, recreation! And mostly out of silliness, stupidity, and narrowness, and if you are to believe them, with the best of intentions. Sometimes I feel like begging them on my knees not to ravage their own insides[6] so brutally.

February 17

I fear my ambassador and I will not put up with each other much longer. The man is utterly unbearable. His way of working and doing business is so ridiculous that I cannot refrain from contradicting him and often doing something in my own way, according to my own idea; and this, of course, he never approves of. For this reason he recently complained about me at the Court, and the minister rebuked me—gently to be sure: still it was a rebuke, and I was on the point of submitting my resignation when I received a private letter from him,[7] a letter which made me kneel down and worship his lofty, noble, wise spirit. How he rebukes my excessive sensitivity, how he respects my exaggerated ideas of efficiency, of influence on others, of getting business done, as youthful ardor, and does not seek to eradicate them, only to soften and direct them into channels where they can really come into play and produce vigorous results. So I have been strengthened for another week and

6. Common eighteenth-century synonym for heart, mind, feelings.

7. The letter in question, and another mentioned below, have been withdrawn from this collection out of respect for this excellent gentleman, because we did not believe that such an impropriety could be excused even by the warmest gratitude of the public [Goethe's note].

have become at one with myself. Peace of mind is a glorious thing and so is joy in oneself. My dear friend, if only this jewel were not as fragile as it is beautiful and precious.

February 20

God bless you, my dear ones, may He give you all the good days He withholds from me.

Thanks, Albert, for deceiving me; I was waiting to hear when the wedding-day would be, and had resolved to take down Lotte's silhouette most solemnly from the wall on that day and to bury it among other papers. Now you are married and her picture is still here. Well, it shall remain here. And why not? I know that I, too, am with you, and in Lotte's heart, without injury to you; I have, yes, I have second place in it and I will and must retain it. Oh, I would go mad if she could forget—Albert, there is hell in that thought. Albert, farewell! Farewell, angel from Heaven—farewell, Lotte!

March 15

I have had an annoying experience which will drive me from here. I am gnashing my teeth. The devil! It can't be undone and you alone are to blame, you who spurred and drove and tormented me to take a position that didn't appeal to me. Serves me right—and you too! And so that you don't say again that my extravagant ideas ruin everything, here is the tale, my dear sir, simple and clear, the way a chronicler would write it down.

Count von C—— likes me, singles me out, you know that—I've told you so a hundred times. Well, I was at his house for dinner yesterday, the very day on which the aristocratic ladies and gentlemen gather at his place in the evening. I hadn't remembered this, and it never occurred to me that we of the lower ranks don't belong there. Well, I dine at the Count's, and after dinner we are walking up and down in the great hall, I'm talking to him, and to Colonel B—— who joins us, and so the hour of the soirée approaches. Heaven knows, I suspect nothing, when in comes supergracious Lady von S—— with Her Consort and Her well-hatched little goose of a daughter with the flat chest and the dainty, laced bodice, *en passant* they turn up their highly aristocratic eyes and nostrils in the usual manner. I heartily detest the whole breed and was on the point of taking my leave, only waiting till the Count had freed himself from the dreadful chatter, when my Fräulein von B—— came in. As I always feel cheered when I see her, I simply stayed on, stood behind her chair and noticed only after a while that she was talking to me with less than her usual frankness, in fact, with some embarrassment. I was perplexed by this. Is she, too, like all the others? I thought. I was nettled and wanted to go but stayed nevertheless because I wanted to find excuses for her, and couldn't believe it, and still hoped for a kind word from her and—anything you please. Meanwhile, the rest of the company arrives. There is Baron F——, dressed entirely in clothes dating from the coronation of Emperor Francis I,[8] Court Councillor R—— (here called Herr von R—— *in qualitate*)[9] with his deaf wife, etc., not to forget the shabbily dressed J——, who repairs the holes in his old-fashioned wardrobe with modern patches. They come in droves, and I talked with some people I know, all of whom were very laconic. I thought—and paid attention only to my Fräulein von B——. I didn't notice that the women were whispering to each other at the end of the drawing room, that the whispering was taken up by the men, that Frau von S—— was talking to the Count (all this I learned later from Fräulein von B——),[1] until finally the Count came up to me and led me to a window. "You know our strange ways," he said; "the company, I notice, is not happy about seeing you here. I would not, for anything in the world. . . ." "Your Excellency, I beg a thousand pardons," I interrupted, "I ought to have thought of it sooner, and I know you will forgive me my untoward behavior. I meant to leave some time ago, but an evil genius kept me here," I added with a smile, and bowed to him. —The Count pressed both my hands with a depth of feeling which spoke eloquently. I quietly slipped away from the distinguished company, took my seat in a cabriolet and drove to M—— to watch the sun set there from the hilltop, and to read that glorious canto in Homer in which Ulysses is entertained by the excellent swineherd.[2] It was a satisfying experience.

In the evening I returned to the inn for dinner, there were only a few people left in the dining room; they had turned back the tablecloth and were playing dice in a corner of the table. Then Adelin, that honest fellow, came in, put down his hat, looked at me, came over and said quietly: "You've had an unpleasant experience?" "I?" I said. "The Count asked you to leave the company." "The devil take them!" I said, "I was glad to get out into the fresh

8. Francis I was crowned emperor of the Holy Roman Empire in 1745.

9. I.e., by virtue of being admitted to this aristocratic society, he was addressed with a title.

1. The following letter tells us that Werther spoke to Fraulein von B—— on March 16, i.e., the next day.

2. Book XIV of the *Odyssey*.

air." —"Good," he said, "that you take the matter lightly; but I'm annoyed, the story has already made the rounds." —It was only then that the matter began to nag at me. Anyone who came to the table and looked at me made me suspect: he's looking at you because of that. That poisoned my blood.

And today, wherever I appear, people pity me, I hear that my enemies are triumphant and say: you see where the arrogant end, those who feel superior because of their bit of intellect and think it entitles them to disregard all convention—and all the rest of this rotten gossip. You feel like plunging a knife into your heart; for say what you wish about independence, I'd like to see the man who can bear to have rogues talk about him when they have him at a disadvantage; if their prattle is empty, well, then you can easily disregard them.

March 16

Everything conspires against me. Today I met Fräulein von B—— on the avenue. I could not resist talking to her and, as soon as we were a little distance from her companions, showing her that I was hurt by her recent behavior. —"Oh Werther," she said in a passionate tone, "can you interpret my confusion in this way when you know my heart? What I suffered for your sake, from the moment I stepped into the drawing room! I saw it all in advance, a hundred times it was on the tip of my tongue to tell you. I knew that that von S—— and T—— and their husbands would sooner leave than remain in your company. I knew that the Count must not break with them—and now all this row!" —"What row, dear lady?" I said, concealing my alarm; for everything Adelin had told me the day before yesterday rushed through my veins at this moment like boiling water. —"What grief it has already caused me," the sweet creature said with tears in her eyes. —I was no longer in control of my emotions, was on the point of throwing myself at her feet. —"Explain yourself," I cried. —The tears ran down her cheeks. I was beside myself. She dried them, without trying to conceal them. —"You know my aunt," she began; "she was there and saw it—oh, with what eyes! Werther, what I endured last night, and this morning[3] I was given a sermon about my association with you, and I had to hear you disparaged and degraded, and I could and dared only half defend you."

---

3. The "incident" occurred on March 14. Adelin reported the rumors that same evening. It seems likely that the poisonous aunt would belabor her niece immediately after the event and deliver her sermon next morning (March 15), not "yesterday" (March 15) and "this morning" (March 16).

Every word she uttered pierced my heart like a sword. She did not feel what an act of mercy it would have been to keep all this from me, and she even added what further gossip would be spread and the sort of people who would feel triumphant about it. How they would now gloat and delight in the punishment of my arrogance and my contempt for others, for which I have long been reproached. To hear all this from her, Wilhelm, in a tone of genuine compassion—I was devastated, and I am still in an inner rage. I wish someone would dare to reproach me, so that I could run my sword through his body; at the sight of blood I would feel better. Oh, I've seized a knife a hundred times, to ease this oppressed heart of mine. I have heard of a noble race of horses which, when they are terribly overheated and excited, instinctively bite into a vein to breathe more freely. So it is often with me, I'd like to open a vein to gain eternal freedom.

March 24

I have asked for my release from the Court and will, I hope, receive it, and you will both pardon me for not obtaining permission from you first. I simply had to get away; I know everything you would say by way of encouraging me to stay and so—Break it gently to mother. I can't help myself and she will have to make the best of the fact that I can't help her either. Of course it's bound to hurt her. To see the beautiful beginning her son had just made toward becoming a privy councillor and ambassador suddenly halted, and back to the stable with the animal! Make what you will of it and calculate the possible situations in which I could and should have stayed on; enough, I'm going, and so that you may know where I'll be, let me tell you that Prince—— is here; he finds much pleasure in my company; when he heard of my intention to resign he asked me to accompany him to his estates and spend the lovely spring there. He promised I would be left entirely to myself, and since we understand each other up to a certain point, I'll take a chance and go with him.

For Your Information
April 19

Thanks for your two letters. I did not reply because I left this sheet blank until my release from the Court was in; I feared mother might write the minister and make my plan more difficult to realize. But now it's happened, my release is here. I don't want to tell you how reluctantly they gave it to me and what the minister writes me—you would break out in new lamentations. The Prince sent me twenty-five ducats as a parting gift, with a note that moved me to tears; so I don't need the money from mother about which I recently wrote.

May 5

I am leaving here tomorrow, and because my birthplace is only six miles out of my way, I'd like to see it again, and recall the old, happy days I dreamed away. I will enter by the very gate from which my mother drove out with me when she left the dear, familiar spot after the death of my father, to shut herself up in her unbearable city. Adieu, Wilhelm, you shall hear about my journey.

May 9

I have completed the pilgrimage to my native town with all the devotion of a pilgrim, and I was gripped by many unexpected emotions. I had the coach stop at the big linden tree that stands about a quarter of an hour's distance from the town in the direction of S——, got out and told the postilion to go on so that I might savor on foot every memory to my heart's content as something quite new and vivid. There I now stood under the linden tree which used to be the goal and boundary of my walks when I was a boy. What a difference now! Then, in the bliss of ignorance, I longed to get out into the unfamiliar world, where I hoped to find so much nourishment, so much enjoyment, for my heart to fulfill my aspirations and to satisfy my yearning. Now I was returning from the great world—oh my friend, with how many frustrated hopes, with how many ruined plans! —The mountains which had a thousand times been the goal of my wishes I saw stretched out before me. I could sit here for hours, longing to be beyond them, to lose myself with all my soul in the forests and valleys that stood before my eyes in such a welcome half light; and when I had to return at the appointed time, how unwillingly I left the beloved spot! —I approached the city and greeted all the old, familiar summerhouses; the new ones displeased me, as did all the other changes that had taken place. I entered the gate and at once felt at home again. Dear friend, I don't want to go into details; it would become as boring in the narration as it was charming to me in reality. I had resolved to lodge in the marketplace, right next to our old house. On my way there I noticed that the schoolhouse in which a good old woman had cooped up our childhood had been converted into a store. I remembered the restlessness, the tears, the mental apathy, the anguish of heart I had endured in that hole. I could not take a single step that was not noteworthy for me. A pilgrim in the Holy Land does not encounter so many scenes of religious memories, and his soul is scarcely so full of sacred emotion. —One more memory to stand for a thousand. I followed the stream to a certain farm; I used to walk this road, and I found the places where we boys used to practice skipping flat stones on the water to see who could make his rebound most often. I recalled so vividly how I sometimes stood there watching the flowing water, with what wonderful hopes I followed it with my eyes, how exciting I imagined the regions to be to which it was now flowing; and how I soon came to the limits of my imaginative powers; and yet it had to go on, on, and on, and I lost myself completely in the contemplation of an invisible distance. —See, my dear friend, the glorious patriarchs were just so limited and so happy; so childlike was their feeling and their poetry! When Ulysses speaks of the boundless sea and the infinite earth, it is so true, so human, so sincere, so constricted, and so mysterious. What good is it to me that I can now repeat with every schoolboy that it is round? Man needs only a few clods of earth to enjoy life on, and fewer still to rest beneath.

Now I am here in the Prince's hunting lodge. It is quite easy to live with the gentleman; he is genuine and simple. Strange people surround him, people I do not understand at all. They don't appear to be rogues and yet they haven't the look of honest men. Sometimes they seem to me to be honest and yet I can't trust them. One thing I regret is that he often speaks of things which he has only heard or read about, and moreover from the point of view from which someone else has chosen to present them.

Besides, he values my intelligence and talents more than my heart, which is really my sole pride, and which alone is the source of everything, of all my strength, all my bliss, and all my misery. Ah, what I know, everyone can know—my heart is mine alone.

May 25

I have been planning something which I did not want to mention until it was accomplished; now that it has come to nothing, I may as well do so. I wanted to go to the wars; I have long cherished the idea. This was the principal reason for my following the Prince to this place, for he is a general in the service of ——. On one of our walks I revealed my plan to him; he advised me against it; if I had not heeded his reasons it would have indicated passion for the idea rather than the whim it was.

June 11

Say what you will, I can't stay here any longer. What am I to do here? Time hangs heavy on my hands. The Prince is treating me as well as anyone could, and yet I don't feel comfortable. Basically we have nothing in common. He is a man of intellect, but of very common intellect; my association with him is no more entertaining than if I were to read a well-written book. I will stay another week and then I'll set out on my wanderings again. The best thing I've done here is my sketching. The Prince has a feeling for art and would be even more sensitive if he were not circumscribed by a horrid concern for theory and traditional terminology. Sometimes I gnash my teeth when I lead him about in nature and art with warm imagination and he suddenly thinks he's helping matters by stumbling in with some hackneyed technical term.

June 16

I am indeed but a wanderer, a pilgrim on earth. But are you anything more?

June 18

Where do I want to go? Let me tell you in confidence. I must stay here another fortnight, and then I've persuaded myself that I want to visit the mines at ———. But there's really no truth in it, I only want to be closer to Lotte, that's all. I laugh at my own heart—and do what it wishes.

July 29

No, it's all right, everything is well. I— her husband! O God, Who did give me life, if You had prepared this happiness for me, my whole existence would be a perpetual prayer. I will not quarrel with You, and forgive me these tears, forgive me my vain desires. She—my wife! If I had held her, the dearest creature under the sun, in my arms—— A shudder goes through my whole body, Wilhelm, when Albert puts his arms about her slender waist.

And dare I say it? Why not, Wilhelm? She would have been happier with me than with him. Oh, he's not the man to fulfill all the wishes of that heart. A certain lack of sensibility, a lack—take

it as you wish, that his heart does not beat in sympathy over—
oh!—over a passage in a favorite book, when my heart and Lotte's
are in harmony; in a hundred other instances when it happens that
our feelings about the behavior of a third person are revealed. Dear
Wilhelm! —Of course he loves her with all his heart, and such a
love deserves everything.—

An unbearable person has interrupted me. My tears are dried. I
am distracted. Adieu, dear friend.

August 4

I am not the only one. All men are disappointed in their hopes,
deceived in their expectations. I visited my good woman under the
linden tree. Her oldest boy ran out to meet me; his cry of joy
brought out his mother, who looked very dejected. Her first words
were: "My dear sir, alas, my Hans has died." —He was the youngest of her boys. I was silent. —"And my husband," she said,
"returned from Switzerland and brought nothing back with him,
and if it weren't for some good people he would have had to beg
his way home, he had contracted a fever on his journey." —I could
say nothing to her and gave the little boy something; she asked me
to accept a few apples, which I did, and I left that place of mournful memory.

August 21

With a turn of the hand my fortunes have changed. Sometimes
a joyful spark of life is about to shine for me again, but alas! only
for a moment. —When I lose myself in dreams, I cannot avoid the
thought: suppose Albert were to die? You would—yes, she
would—and then I pursue this chimera until it leads me to abysses
from which I shrink back.

When I walk out of the town gate, on the road I traveled the
first time to fetch Lotte for the dance, how different it was then.
Everything, everything has passed by. No trace of that former
world, not a throb of the emotion I felt then. My condition is that
of a ghost who returned to the burnt-out, ruined castle he had once
built, equipped with all the gifts of splendor, when he was a flour-
ishing prince, leaving it, at his death, full of hope to his beloved
son.

September 3

Sometimes I cannot understand how another man can love her,
dare love her, since I love her so wholly, so fervently, so fully, and
recognize nothing and know nothing, and have nothing but her!

September 4

Yes, it is so. As nature declines into autumn, so autumn begins within me and about me. My leaves are turning yellow and the leaves of the neighboring trees have already fallen. Didn't I write you once about a peasant boy, soon after I got here? I've made inquiries about him again at Wahlheim; they told me he has been driven from his job and no one wanted to have anything more to do with him. Yesterday I met him by chance on the road to another village; I spoke to him and he told me his story, which has moved me doubly and triply, as you will easily understand when I pass it on to you. But why all this? Why don't I keep to myself what causes me anxiety and grief?[4] Why do I sadden you as well and why do I always give you opportunities for pitying and blaming me? Let us say, this too is perhaps part of my fate.

At first the lad answered my questions with a quiet melancholy, in which I thought I noticed a bit of shyness; but very soon he spoke more frankly, as if he suddenly recognized himself and me again; he admitted his faults to me and lamented his misfortune. If only I could, my friend, put every one of his words to your judgment! He confessed, indeed he told me with a sort of delight and happiness in remembering that the passion for his employer had grown in him daily, until at last he didn't know what he was doing, nor, as he expressed it, where to turn his head. He hadn't been able to eat, drink, or sleep; he had had a lump in his throat, had done what he should not have done, had forgotten the orders that were given him; it was as if he had been pursued by an evil demon, until one day, when he knew that she was in an upstairs room, he had followed her, or rather been drawn after her; when she refused to grant his wishes, he tried to take her by force, he didn't know what had come over him, and took God to witness that his intentions toward her had always been honorable and that he had wished for nothing more fervently than that she should marry him and spend her life with him. After he had talked a while he began to hesitate, like a person who has something more to say but does not dare utter it; finally he confessed to me shyly the little intimacies she had permitted him and how much familiarity she had granted him. He broke off two or three times and repeated, with the most vehement protestations, that he was not saying this to put her in a bad light, as he expressed it, that he loved and esteemed her as before,

---

4. The German text has *kränkt*—offends. But Erich Trunz, one of the best modern editors, argues that the word means "sickens" in this context and refers to page 34, line 38 and to page 39, the opening line of the letter of August 28.

that these words had never crossed his lips, he was telling me all this only to convince me that he was not totally depraved and mad. —And at this point, my dear friend, I must begin the old song again, which I shall always sing: if I could only place the man before you as he stood before me, as he still stands before me. If I could express everything precisely, so that you might feel how much I sympathize, must sympathize, with his fate. But enough, since you know my fate too, and know me too, you know only too well what it is that draws me to all unhappy people, and especially to this unhappy man.

As I read this page through again, I see that I forgot to tell the end of the story; but you can easily imagine it. She resisted him; her brother appeared, who had long hated him and had wanted him out of the house for a long time because he fears that if his sister marries again, his own children will lose the inheritance, which now rouses high hopes in them, as she is childless. The brother had driven him out of the house on the spot and made such a fuss about the matter that the woman could not have taken him back even if she had wanted to. He has heard that she has hired another man since and that she has quarreled with her brother about this man too; people are certain that she will marry him, and he is firmly resolved not to survive that day.

What I am telling you is not exaggerated, not sentimentalized at all; indeed, I may say that I have told it feebly, very feebly, and I have coarsened it by couching it in our traditional moral terms.

This love, this faithfulness, this passion is, then, not an invention of poets. It exists, and it is purest in that class of people whom we call uncultivated, rude—we who are formed by culture and deformed[5] into nobodies! Please read this story with reverence. I am calm today as I write this down; you see from my handwriting that I am not boiling and bubbling as usual. Read it, my dear friend, and think as you read that it is also the story of your friend. Yes, this has happened to me, this will happen to me, and I am not half so worthy nor half so resolute as that poor, unhappy man, with whom I hardly dare compare myself.

September 5

She had written a note to her husband in the country, where he was on business. It began: "My dearest and best, come as soon as you can, I await you with a thousand joys." —A friend who came

5. A play on *gebildet*, cultivated and *verbildet*, miseducated, deformed, i.e., our education ruins us—"Rousseauism."

in brought the news that Albert would not come back so soon because of certain circumstances. The note was not sent and fell into my hands that evening. I read it and smiled; she asked me why. "What a divine gift is imagination," I exclaimed, "for a moment I was able to imagine that it was written to me." —She dropped the subject, it seemed to displease her, so I kept quiet.

September 6

It was a difficult decision for me to abandon my simple blue dress coat in which I first danced with Lotte, but it was becoming quite threadbare. Besides, I had had one made exactly like it, even to the collar and facings, and another yellow vest and trousers to go with it.

But it doesn't produce quite the same effect. I don't know—I think in time I'll get to like it better.

September 12

She has been away for a few days to fetch Albert. Today I entered her room; she came toward me and I kissed her hand, overjoyed.

A canary flew from the mirror to her shoulder. "A new friend," she said, coaxing it on to her hand. "I got him for the children. Isn't he adorable? Look at him! When I give him bread he flutters his wings and pecks so nicely. He kisses me too, you see?"

When she held out her lips to the little creature, it pressed against her sweet lips so charmingly, as if it could feel the bliss it was enjoying.

"He shall kiss you too," she said and handed me the bird. —The little beak made its way from her lips to mine, and the peck was like a breath, a foretaste of the delights of love.

"His kiss," I said, "is not entirely free from greed, he is seeking nourishment and returns to you unsatisfied by the empty caress."

"He also takes food from my mouth," she said. —She gave him a few crumbs with her lips, on which the joys of an innocently shared love smiled delightfully.

I averted my face. She should not do this! She should not excite my imagination with these pictures of heavenly innocence and bliss, nor wake my heart out of the sleep into which the indifference of life sometimes lulls it. —And why not? —She trusts me so! She knows how much I love her.

September 15

It makes me furious, Wilhelm, that there are people without understanding or feeling for the few things on earth that still have value. You know the nut trees under which I sat with Lotte at the home of the worthy parson of St——,[5a] those splendid nut trees! which, Heaven knows, always filled me with profound happiness! How cozy they made the parsonage, how cool, and how splendid their branches were! And the memory they carried of the worthy clergymen who planted them so many years ago. The schoolmaster often mentioned the name of one of them, which he had heard from his grandfather; and he is said to have been such a fine man, and his memory was always sacred to me under the trees. I tell you the tears stood in the schoolmaster's eyes when we talked yesterday about the fact that they had been cut down. —Cut down! I could go mad, I could murder the dog who struck the first blow at them. I, who could die of grief if such a pair of trees stood in my yard and one of them died of old age, I must stand by and look at this. But, my dear fellow, there's at least one thing about it. The power of human feeling! The whole village is muttering, and I hope the pastor's wife will be made to feel what a wound she has dealt the place, in the butter and eggs and the other tokens of esteem she receives. For she's the one, the wife of the new pastor (the old one died), a skinny, sickly creature who has good reason for showing no interest in the world, since no one shows any interest in her. A foolish woman, who affects to be learned and meddles in the investigations concerning the canonical books,[6] works hard on the new-fangled moral-critical reformation of Christianity, and shrugs her shoulders at Lavater's enthusiasms.[7] Her health is quite broken and so she experiences no joy on God's earth. Only such a creature could possibly have cut down my nut trees. You see, I can't regain control of myself! Just imagine, the falling leaves make her yard messy and damp, the trees shut out the light, and when the nuts are ripe the boys throw stones at them and this gets on her nerves, disturbs her profound meditation when she is weighing the merits of Kennicott, Semler, and Michaelis[8] against one another. When I

5a. See page 21.

6. Eighteenth-century liberal theology examined the books of the Bible critically to determine which of them are canonical, i.e., divine and authoritative.

7. Lavater's general position in theology is antirationalist. He was a friend of Hamann, Herder, and the young Goethe. The rationalistic Frau Pfarre-

rin would therefore shrug her shoulders at his "enthusiasms."

8. Benjamin Kennicott (1718–1783), British scholar, wrote critically on the text of the Old Testament; J. S. Semler (1725–1791) tried to establish a canon of the Biblical books; J. D. Michaelis (1717–1791) published a critical translation of the Old Testament.

saw that the people in the village were so dissatisfied, expecially the old ones, I said, "Why did you permit it?" "In these parts," they replied, "if the mayor is willing, what can you do?" —But one good thing happened. The mayor and the pastor, who after all wanted to gain some advantage from his wife's notions—which usually add no nourishment to his soup—intended to divide the trees between them. But the treasury learned of it and said: "This way!" for it still had some old claims on that part of the parsonage in which the trees had stood, and sold them to the highest bidder. They are down! Oh, if I were a Prince! I would have the pastor's wife, the mayor, and the treasury—a Prince! Yes, if I were a Prince, what would I care about the trees in my domain?

October 10

I have only to look into her black eyes to feel happy. And what annoys me is that Albert does not seem to be as happy as he—hoped—as I—thought I would have been—if—I don't like to use dashes, but in this instance I can't express myself in any other way—and it seems to me they are clear enough.

October 12

Ossian[9] has displaced Homer in my heart. What a world it is into which the glorious poet leads me! To wander over the heath, with the tempestuous winds roaring about you, carrying the spirits of your ancestors in steaming mists by the half light of the moon. To hear the dying groans of the spirits issue from their caves in the mountains, amid the roar of the brook in the forest, and the lamentations of the maiden, grieving her life away by the four moss-covered, grass-overgrown stones on the tomb of her lover, nobly slain in battle. When I then find him, the wandering, gray-haired bard, who is seeking the footsteps of his fathers on the broad heath, but finds, alas, only their tombstones and then gazes in misery at the beloved evening star which takes refuge in the rolling sea; and the memory of past ages comes alive in the hero's soul,

9. Ossian, the legendary Gaelic bard of the third century A.D. Supposed translations from his works were published by James Macpherson (1736–1796): *Fragments of Ancient Poetry* (1760), *Fingal* (1762), *Temora* (1763), in a collected edition (1765). These gloomy ballads and songs were taken for genuine translations and acclaimed throughout Europe. Macpherson's imposture was not proven till 1840, though some (e.g., Samuel Johnson) had their suspicions. Klopstock, Herder, and the young Goethe were Ossian enthusiasts. Goethe translated some of the Ossian songs into German. See page 84, line 6.

when the friendly light still shone on the perils of the brave and the moon lit their garlanded ship returning victorious. When I read the deep sorrow on his brow, and see the last of the glorious men as he totters, lonely and feeble, to the grave and draws ever new and painfully burning joys from the powerless presence of the shadows of his departed ones, and looks down on the cold earth and the tall, waving grass and exclaims: "The wanderer will come who knew me in my beauty, and will ask, 'Where is the bard, Fingal's admirable son?' His footsteps will pass over my grave, and he will ask in vain after me on earth."[1] —Oh, my friend! Then I would like to draw my sword like a noble warrior, to liberate my Prince with one stroke from the quivering torment of a slowly ebbing life, and send my soul to follow the liberated demigod.

October 19

Oh, this void, this dreadful void which I feel here in my bosom! —I often think: if you could only once, just once, press her to this heart, this whole void would be filled.

October 26

Yes, I'm beginning to feel certain, dear friend, certain and ever more certain that the life of a human creature matters little, very little. One of Lotte's friends came in to see her and I went into the next room to fetch a book, but I could not read, and then I took a pen to write. I heard them talking softly; they were telling each other insignificant trifles, town gossip: how this one was getting married, that one was sick, very sick. "She has a dry cough, her cheekbones protrude, and she has fainting spells; I wouldn't give a penny for her life," said the friend. "So and So is in a bad way too," said Lotte. "He's all swollen up," said the other girl. —And my lively imagination transported me to the bedsides of these poor people; I saw them turn their backs on life with the utmost repugnance, saw them—and Wilhelm, my little ladies were talking about it, well, as one would talk—about the death of a stranger. —And when I look about me and examine the room, with Lotte's dresses and Albert's papers around me, and this furniture which is so familiar to me, even to this inkwell—and I think: see what you now mean to this family—all in all! Your friends respect you; you often give them pleasure, and your heart feels as if it could not exist without them, and yet—if you went now, if you left this sphere,

---

1. The quotation is from the passage of Ossian quoted on page 88, lines 20 ff.

would they feel, how long would they feel the gap which your loss has torn in their destiny? How long? —Oh, man is so transitory that he must vanish even where he enjoys complete certainty of his existence, where he makes the only true impression of his presence in the memory, in the soul of his loved ones, even there he must be extinguished and vanish, and that so soon!

October 27

I often feel like tearing out my heart and bashing in my brains at the thought that we mean so little to each other. Alas, the love, joy, warmth, and bliss which I do not contribute myself, no one else will give me, and even with a heart full of happiness I will not make anyone happy who stands before me cold and indifferent.

October 27, evening

I have so much, yet my feeling for her devours everything; I have so much, and without her it all turns to nothing.

October 30

A hundred times I have been on the point of throwing my arms about her. The good Lord knows how it feels to see so much charm cruising around before one and not dare to touch it; and yet to touch is man's most natural impulse. Don't children touch everything they see? —And I?

November 3

Heaven knows, I often go to bed with the wish, sometimes even with the hope, that I shall not awaken again; and the next morning I open my eyes, see the sun again and am miserable. Oh, I wish I could be moody, blame the weather or someone else or some undertaking that has failed; then the unbearable burden of my resentment would only half rest on me. Woe is me! I feel it is only too true that the fault is all mine—not fault! It is enough that the source of all my wretchedness is buried in myself, as the source of all my happiness was at one time. For am I not still the same person who once floated about in the abundance of his emotions, whom paradise followed everywhere, who had a heart that could embrace a whole world with love? And this heart is now dead, no raptures flow from it any longer; my eyes are dry and my faculties,[2] no longer invigorated by refreshing tears, cause my brow to be knitted in anxiety. I suffer much, for I have lost what was the sole joy of my life: the sacred, animating force with which I created worlds about me; it is gone! —When I look out from my window toward the distant hill, how the morning sun breaks through the mist above it and illuminates the tranquil meadow in the valley, and the gentle river winds its way toward me between its leafless willows—oh! when this magnificent scene stands before me as stiff as a lacquered little painting and all this bliss cannot pump one drop of happiness from my heart into my brain, and the whole man stands before the countenance of God like a dried-up spring, like a leaky pail. I have often thrown myself to the ground and begged God for tears, as a farmer begs for rain when the sky above him is brazen and the earth about him is parched.

But alas! I feel it, God does not grant rain and sunshine to our impetuous requests, and those bygone days, the memory of which torments me so, why were they so happy except because I waited for His spirit with patience, and received the bliss which He poured out over me with an undivided, fervently grateful heart!

November 8

She has reproached me for my excesses, ah, with such kindness! My excesses, that I sometimes allow myself to be tempted by a glass of wine to drink a whole bottle. —"Don't do it," she said, "think of Lotte." —"Think of you!" I said, "Do you have to bid me to do that? I think—I don't think. You are always in my mind. Today I was sitting on the spot where you recently got out of the carriage——" She changed the subject, to prevent me from getting deeper into this one. My dear friend, I am lost, she can do what she pleases with me.

November 15[3]

I thank you, Wilhelm, for your cordial sympathy, for your well-meant advice, and I beg you to be at ease. Let me suffer to the end; with all my weariness I still have enough strength to hold out. I respect religion, you know that; I feel that it is a staff for many a weary man, a refreshment for many a parched throat. Only—can it, must it be that for everyone? If you look at the great world, you will see thousands for whom it has not been so, thousands for

---

2. The German text has *Sinne*, senses—probably, inner senses.
3. This letter is rich in Biblical allusions, comparing Werther's suffering to that of Christ on the Cross. See Afterword, p. 111.

whom it will not be so, whether it is preached or not preached; and must it then be so for me? Does not the Son of God Himself say that they shall be His whom the Father has given to Him?[4] Well, what if I have not been given to Him? What if the Father wants to keep me for Himself, as my heart tells me? —Please do not misinterpret this; do not, for instance, see mockery in these innocent words; it is my whole soul that I bare before you; otherwise I would wish I had been silent, as I don't like to waste words on matters about which people know as little as I do. What else is it but human destiny to suffer one's measure to the end, to drain one's cup —And if the cup became too bitter on the human lips of God from Heaven, why should I brag and pretend that it tastes sweet to me? And why should I feel shame in the terrible moment when my whole existence trembles between being and nonbeing, when my past is illuminated like lightning over the dark abyss of the future, and everything about me is swallowed up, and the world perishes with me? —Is it not the voice of the creature, thrown completely upon itself, insufficient unto itself, plunging inevitably to destruction, that moans from the innermost depth, laboring in vain to reach the surface: "My God, my God, why hast Thou forsaken me?" And should I feel ashamed to utter these words, should I fear the moment,[5] when even He Who rolls up the heavens like a cloth[6] did not escape it?

November 21

She does not see, she does not feel that she is preparing a poison that will destroy both me and her; and voluptuously I drain the cup which she hands me for my destruction. What good are the kind looks she often gives me—often?—no, not often, but at least sometimes; the favor with which she receives some involuntary expression of my feelings, the compassion for my suffering which is marked on her brow?

Yesterday when I went away she gave me her hand and said: "Adieu, dear Werther!" Dear Werther! It was the first time she called me "dear," and it pierced me to the marrow. I have repeated it to myself a hundred times, and last night, as I was about to retire and was chattering away to myself, I suddenly said: "Good night, dear Werther," and then had to laugh at myself.

4. John 6:37, 44, 66.
5. Werther is not justifying his fear of death, but his condemnation of life. "Shall I lack the courage to say at the last moment: life is not worth living, when Jesus Himself said as much?"
6. Psalms 104:2.

November 22

I cannot pray, "Let her be mine!" and yet she often seems to me to be mine. I cannot pray, "Give her to me!" for she belongs to another. I mock my own suffering; if I were to let myself go, the result would be a whole litany of antitheses.

November 24

She feels what I suffer. Today she gave me a look that penetrated deep into my heart. I found her alone; I said nothing, and she looked at me. And I no longer saw in her face the lovely beauty, no longer the radiance of her excellent mind; all that vanished before my eyes. A far more glorious look from her eyes affected me, filled with the expression of the most tender sympathy, the sweetest compassion. Why could I not throw myself at her feet? Why could I not take her in my arms and reply to her with a thousand kisses? She took refuge at the piano and in a sweet, low voice accompanied her playing with harmonious sounds. Never have I seen her lips so charming; it was as if they opened thirsting, to drink in those sweet tones that flowed from the instrument, as if only a mysterious echo reverberated from her pure lips. —Oh, if only I could express this to you in words! —I could resist no longer, I bent forward and swore: I will never dare to imprint a kiss upon you, you lips on which the heavenly spirits hover. —And yet—I will—Ha! you see, this stands like a barrier before my soul—this bliss—and then destruction, in atonement for this sin—sin?

November 26

Sometimes I tell myself: Your fate is unique; consider other men fortunate—no one has ever been tormented like this. Then I read some poet of ancient times and I feel as if I were looking into my own heart. I have so much to endure! Ah, have men before me ever been so wretched?

November 30

I cannot, I cannot recover. Wherever I go I meet an apparition that robs me of all my composure. Today—oh, destiny! Oh, humanity!

I was walking by the river at noon and felt no desire to eat. Everything was desolate, a cold, moist evening wind was blowing from the mountain, and gray rain clouds were moving into the valley. From a distance I saw a man in a shabby green coat crawling about among the rocks, apparently looking for herbs. When I came closer to him and he turned around because of the noise I made, I saw a most interesting face, whose chief feature was a quiet sorrow, but which otherwise expressed nothing but straightforward decency. His black hair was done in two rolls held by pins, the rest plaited in a thick pigtail which hung down his back. As his dress seemed to indicate a man of humble rank, I thought he would not resent it if I showed an interest in what he was doing, so I asked him what he was looking for. "I look for flowers," he replied with a deep sigh, "but find none." —"But it isn't the season for them," I said with a smile. —"There are so many flowers," he said, coming down to me. "In my garden there are roses and two species of honeysuckle, one was given to me by my father, they grow like weeds, I have been looking for them for two days and can't find them. There are always flowers out here, yellow and blue and red, and the centaury has a lovely flower. But I can't find a single one of them." —I noticed that there was something weird about him, so I asked in a roundabout way: "What do you want the flowers for?" —A strange, trembling smile distorted his face. —"If you won't give me away," he said, pressing his finger to his lips, "I've promised my girl a bouquet." —"That's nice," I said. —"Oh," he said, "she has many other things; she's rich." —"And yet she appreciates your bouquet," I added. —"Oh," he continued, "she has jewels and a crown." —"And what is her name?" —"If the Estates General[7] would pay me," he replied, "I'd be a different man. Yes, there was a time when I was so happy! Now it's all over with me. Now I am . . ." A tearful glance to heaven told everything. —"So you were happy?" I asked. —"Oh, I wish I were again," he said. "At that time I was as happy, as merry, as light as a fish in water." —"Heinrich," cried an old woman who was walking along the road, "Heinrich, where are you? We've been looking for you everywhere; come and eat." —"Is that your son?" I asked, going up to her. —"My poor son, indeed," she replied. "God has given me a heavy cross to bear." —"How long has he been like this?" I asked. —"He has been as gentle as this for half a year," she said. "Thank heaven he's come this far at last; before that he was raving mad for a whole year, he lay in chains in the madhouse. Now he doesn't harm anyone but he always talks of consorting with kings and emperors. He was such a good, quiet person, who helped support me, he wrote such a beautiful hand; but suddenly he began to

7. The Netherlands government is meant; it was considered to be fabulously rich.

brood, fell into a violent fever, from that into raving madness, and now he is as you see him. If I were to tell you, sir——" I interrupted the stream of her words with the question: "What period of time was it that he talks about so fondly, when he was so happy, so well off?" "The silly boy," she exclaimed with a compassionate smile, "he means the time when he was out of his mind, he's always praising that; that's the time when he was in the madhouse, when he knew nothing about his condition." —This struck me like a thunderclap, I pressed a coin into her hand and left her in haste.

"When you were happy!" I exclaimed, walking swiftly toward the city, "when you felt as happy as a fish in water!" —Lord in Heaven! Have You so decreed men's fate that they are happy only before they attain the state of reason and after they have lost it again? —Wretched man! And yet how I envy your melancholy, the confusion of your senses in which you are languishing. You start out hopefully to pick flowers for your queen—in winter—and feel sad when you find none, and don't understand why you can't find any. And I—and I go out without hope, without purpose, and return home in the same spirit. —You imagine what sort of person you would be if the Estates General paid you a salary. Happy creature, who can ascribe your unhappiness to an earthly obstacle! You don't feel! You don't feel that your misery, for which all the kings on earth can do nothing to help you, is rooted in your devastated heart, in your deranged brain.

May he perish without consolation who scoffs at a sick man traveling to the remotest spring which will only increase his sickness and make his death more painful; or who feels superior to the man with a troubled heart who undertakes a pilgrimage to the Holy Sepulcher to rid himself of his bad conscience and to seek relief for his anguished soul. Every footstep over an untrodden road that cuts into his soles is a drop of comfort for his anguished soul, and with every day's journey that he endures, his heart goes to rest relieved of many anxieties. —And you dare call this madness, you phrasemongers, lolling on your soft cushions? —Madness! —O Lord! You see my tears! You Who created man so wretched, why did You also have to provide him with brothers who rob him of even that bit of wretchedness and the bit of trust he has in You, in You, You all-loving One? For what is trust in the virtue of a healing root or in the tears of the vine but trust in You, that You have placed in everything around us the power of healing and relieving which we have need of at every hour? Father, Whom I do not know! Father, Who once filled my whole soul but now turn Your countenance from me, call me to You; be silent no longer! Your silence will not deter this thirsting soul. —And could a man, a father, be angry if his son returned unexpectedly, threw his arms about his neck, and cried: "I am back, father! Be not angry because I cut short my journey, which it was your will that I should endure longer. The world is the same everywhere: toil and effort, followed by reward and joy; but what meaning has that for me? I feel happy only where you are, and in your presence I want to suffer and enjoy." —And You, dear, heavenly Father, would You turn him away?

December 1

Wilhelm! the man about whom I wrote you, that man who was so happy in his unhappiness, was a clerk in the service of Lotte's father, and a passion for her which he nourished, concealed, and then disclosed, causing him to be dismissed from his position, drove him mad. Feel, as you read these dry words, with what derangement this story gripped me when Albert told it to me as calmly as you may be reading it now!

December 4

I beg of you—you see, it's all over with me, I can bear it no longer! Today I was sitting beside her—as I sat, she played the piano, various tunes, and with what expression, what expression! What would you expect? —Her little sister sat on my lap dressing her doll. Tears came to my eyes. I bent down, caught sight of her wedding ring—and my tears flowed—and suddenly she fell into that old, divinely sweet melody,[8] as if by chance, and a feeling of comfort passed through my heart, and a memory of the past, of the times when I had heard that song, of the gloomy intervals of vexation, of frustrated hopes; and then—I walked up and down the room, my heart suffocating under the pressure. —"For heaven's sake," I said, moving toward her with a vehement outburst, "for heaven's sake, stop!" —She stopped and looked at me blankly. —"Werther," she said with a smile that pierced me to the soul, "Werther, you are very ill; your favorite dishes disagree with you. Go. I beg you, calm yourself." I tore myself away from her and—God, You see my misery and will put an end to it.

December 6

How her form pursues me! Whether I am awake or dreaming,

8. See page 27, line 15.

she fills my mind wholly. When I close my eyes, here in my brain, where my inner vision is concentrated, her black eyes are before me. Here, I can't express it to you in words. If I close my eyes, they are there; like an ocean, like an abyss they lie before me, in me, fill my inner senses.

What is man, that vaunted demigod? Do not his powers fail him precisely where he needs them most? And when he soars in joy or sinks in suffering, is he not arrested in both, brought back to dull, cold consciousness at the very moment when he yearns to lose himself in the plenitude of the infinite?

The Editor to the Reader

How I wish that there were enough testimony about our friend's last extraordinary days in his own hand, so that I should not find it necessary to interrupt by a narrative the sequence of the letters he left.

I have made an effort to gather precise information from the lips of those who were in a position to know his story well. It is a simple story, and all accounts of it agree except for a few slight details. Opinions differ and judgments are divided only on the mental state of the principal actors involved.

What is left for us but to narrate conscientiously what we have learned after repeated efforts, to insert the letters left by the departed one, and not to disregard even the most trivial slip of paper that has turned up, especially since it is so difficult to discover the true and authentic motives for even a single act performed by people who are not of the common run?

Discouragement and apathy had struck ever deeper root in Werther's mind, had become more firmly intertwined, and had gradually taken possession of his whole being. The harmony of his spirit was completely destroyed; an inner burning and vehemence which churned up all his natural powers produced the most objectionable effects and finally left him with only an exhaustion against which he struggled even more fearfully than he had until now fought against all his misery. The growing anxiety in his heart consumed the other faculties of his mind, his vivacity, his alertness; he became a sad social companion, more and more unhappy and more and more unjust as his unhappiness grew. At least this is what Albert's friends say; they assert that Werther was unable to appreciate the pure, serene man who had achieved a degree of happiness for which he had long yearned nor his behavior, which was designed to maintain this happiness for the future too; whereas he consumed his whole substance every day as it were, only to spend the evening in suffering and starvation. Albert, they say, had not changed in this short span of time; he was still the same person whom Werther had known in the beginning, whom he esteemed and honored so highly. He loved Lotte above all else; he was proud of her and wished her to be recognized by everyone as the most glorious being. Could he, then, be blamed for wishing to avert even the shadow of suspicion, or for his unwillingness to share this precious possession with anyone at this moment, even in the most innocent way? They admit that Albert often left his wife's room when Werther was with her, although not out of hatred or dislike for his friend, but only because he felt that his presence was oppressive to Werther.

Lotte's father, who was confined to his room by sickness, sent his carriage for her and she drove out to see him. It was a fine winter day, the first heavy snow had fallen, covering the whole region.

Werther followed her the next morning to escort her back home in case Albert did not come to fetch her.

The clear weather had little effect on his gloomy state of mind; a heavy weight lay on his heart, melancholy fancies had taken a firm grip on him, and his spirit could only move from one painful thought to the next.

As he lived in eternal discord with himself, so the state of others only seemed to him the more dubious and confused; he thought he had disturbed the beautiful relationship between Albert and his wife; he reproached himself for it, and into these reproaches there crept a secret resentment toward the husband.

His thoughts turned to this subject again on his way to Lotte. Yes, yes, he said to himself, gnashing his teeth, this is the intimate, friendly, tender association that extends to everything, this is calm, steadfast loyalty! Surfeit and indifference—that's what it is! Does not every wretched business matter have more attraction for him than his dear, precious wife? Does he appreciate his good fortune? Is he able to give her the respect she deserves? She is his—very well, she is his—I know it, as I know certain other things; I believe I am accustomed to the thought, but it will drive me mad yet, it will destroy me. —And has his friendship for me really stood the test? Doesn't he already regard my attachment to Lotte as an infringement on his rights, my attentions to her as a silent reproach? I know quite well, I feel it, he doesn't like to see me, he wants me to leave, my presence is a burden to him.

He often slackened his swift pace, often stopped in his tracks as if to turn back; but he always directed his steps forward again, and finally, absorbed in such thoughts and soliloquies, he arrived at the hunting lodge, in spite of himself as it were.

He stepped into the doorway and asked for the old gentleman and Lotte; he found the house in some commotion. The oldest boy told him that over in Wahlheim there had been an accident, a peasant had been slain. —This made no special impression on him. —He entered the living room and found Lotte busy pleading with the old gentleman who, in spite of his illness, wanted to go to Wahlheim to investigate the crime on the spot. The culprit was still unknown, the slain man had been found at his own front door in the morning; there was speculation: the murdered man had been in the service of a widow who had formerly had another man in her employ who had left her in a disgruntled frame of mind.

When Werther heard this, he started vehemently. —"Is it possible!" he exclaimed, "I must go there, I can't wait a moment." —He hurried toward Wahlheim; his memory recalled every detail; he did not doubt for a moment that the deed had been committed by the man with whom he had spoken quite often and whom he had come to like so much.

As he had to walk past the linden trees to get to the tavern where the body had been placed, he was horrified at the appearance of the square which had formerly been so dear to him. The threshold where the neighbor's children had so often played was stained with blood. Love and loyalty, the most beautiful of human emotions, had turned into violence and murder. The mighty trees stood leafless and covered with hoarfrost; the beautiful hedges which formed an arch over the low churchyard wall were stripped of foliage, and the tombstones capped with snow looked out through the gaps.

As he approached the tavern, in front of which the whole village was assembled, he suddenly heard shouting. From a distance a band of armed men could be seen, and everyone shouted that the murderer was being brought. Werther looked and did not long remain in doubt. Yes, it was the hired man who had loved the widow so passionately and whom he had encountered some time ago nursing his silent anger, his secret despair.

"What crime have you committed, unhappy man!" Werther exclaimed as he went toward the prisoner. —The man looked at him silently, then replied quite calmly, "No one will have her, she will have no one." —The prisoner was taken into the tavern and Werther hurried away.

This terrible, violent contact had shaken him completely. For a moment he was wrenched out of his sadness, his discontent, his apathetic indifference; an unconquerable feeling of sympathy took possession of him and he was seized by an indescribable desire to save the man. He felt him to be so unhappy, found him so innocent even as a criminal, and identified himself so completely with him that he was certain he could convince others too. He wished to be able to speak at once in his defense, the most eloquent plea was already forming on his lips; he hurried to the hunting lodge and could not refrain from speaking half aloud all that he intended to say before the magistrate.

When he entered the living room, he found Albert present; this put him out of sorts for a moment, but he soon recovered himself and spoke his mind passionately to the magistrate. The latter shook his head a few times, and although Werther, with the utmost animation, passion, and truth, said everything that one man can say in defense of another, the magistrate, as can be easily imagined, was not moved by it. On the contrary, he interrupted our friend in his discourse, contradicted him warmly and rebuked him for protecting a murderer. He showed him that in this way all law would be annulled, the security of the state destroyed, and he added that in such a matter he could do nothing without shouldering the greatest responsibility; everything had to proceed in an orderly manner and take its prescribed course.

Werther did not give up, and merely begged the magistrate to look the other way if the man were helped to escape. But this too the magistrate rejected. Albert, who finally joined the conversation, took the old man's side. Werther was outvoted, and with horrible suffering he went on his way after the magistrate told him several times: "No, he can't be saved!"

How deeply these words must have struck him we can see from a note that was found among his papers and which had quite certainly been written that same day:

"You cannot be saved, unhappy man. I see clearly that we cannot be saved."

Albert's last remarks, uttered in the presence of the magistrate, concerning the prisoner, Werther had found to be most repugnant; he thought he had noticed some resentment against himself in them; and although, upon reflection, his reason told him that the two men might be right, it still seemed to him that he would have to deny his deepest being if he confessed it, if he conceded it.

A note referring to this, which perhaps expresses his whole relationship to Albert, was found among his papers:

"What good is it for me to say to myself over and over again, he is a good and nice man? It tears my heart; I cannot be just."

Because it was a mild evening and the weather was beginning to approach a thaw, Lotte and Albert returned on foot. On the way she looked around here and there, as if she missed Werther's company. Albert began to speak of him; he criticized him but was just to him. He touched on his unhappy passion and wished it were possible to send him away. —"I wish it for our sake too," he said, "and I beg of you," he continued, "try to give his behavior toward you a different direction, see to it that his visits become less frequent. People are beginning to notice, and I know that there has been talk about it here and there." —Lotte was silent and Albert seems to have sensed the meaning of her silence; at least from then on he did not mention Werther to her again, and when she mentioned him, he dropped the conversation or changed the subject.

The futile attempt that Werther had made to save the unfortunate man was the last flicker of a dying light; he sank ever deeper into pain and inactivity. He was almost beside himself when he heard that he might actually be called as a witness against the man, who now denied everything.

All the unpleasant experiences of his active[9] life, the annoying incident at the embassy, every one of his other failures, everything that had offended him kept going through his mind. He seemed to feel that all this justified his inactivity; he found himself cut off from every prospect, unable to get a grip anywhere on the affairs of everyday life; and so, wholly absorbed in his fantastic emotions, his thoughts, and his boundless passion, in the eternal monotony of a melancholy association with the charming and beloved creature whose peace he was destroying, ravaging his energies, exhausting them without purpose or prospect, he moved ever closer to a sorrowful end.

A few letters he left behind offer the strongest evidence of his confusion and passion, his restless activity and exertion, of his weariness with life; we will insert them here.

"December 12

"Dear Wilhelm: My state of mind is like that of the unfortunate creatures of whom it was believed that they were possessed by an evil spirit. Sometimes I have a seizure; it is not anxiety, not longing—it is an unfamiliar, inner raging which threatens to tear my heart asunder and constricts my throat. Woe! Woe! And then I roam about in the terrible nocturnal scenes of this inhuman season.

"Last night I had to go out. A thaw had suddenly set in; I had

9. *Wirksam*, i.e., when he held an office.

heard that the river had overflowed its banks, that all the brooks
were swollen, and that from Wahlheim down my beloved valley
was flooded. After eleven at night I hurried out. A fearful spectacle: to see the turbulent waters eddying down from the rocks in the
moonlight, over fields and meadows and hedges, and all this, up
and down the broad valley, forming one stormy sea in the roaring
of the wind. And then when the moon came out again, resting
above the black clouds, and before me the waters rolled and roared
in the fearful, magnificent reflection, a shudder overcame me and
once more I felt a yearning. I stood with open arms facing the
abyss, whispering, 'down, down,' and was lost in the bliss of fling-
ing my torments and my suffering down there, so that they would
roar like the waves! Oh—but you couldn't lift your foot from the
ground and put an end to all your torments![1] —My time has not
yet run out, I feel it! Oh, Wilhelm, how gladly would I have
yielded my human existence to rend the clouds and grasp the waves
like that tempestuous wind! Ha! And will not the imprisoned man
some day perhaps share in this bliss?—

"And as I looked down sadly on a little spot where I had rested
with Lotte under a willow tree, when we felt hot on one of our
strolls—it was flooded too, and I could barely recognize the willow,
Wilhelm. And her meadows, I thought, the country around her
hunting lodge, how our arbor has been ravaged by the raging river!
And the sunshine of the past looked in on me like a dream of
herds, meadows, and dignities upon a prisoner. But I stood there.
—I do not blame myself, for I have the courage to die. —I
might—Now I am sitting here like an old woman who gathers her
wood from hedgerows and begs her bread from door to door to prolong and ease her joyless, waning existence for one moment more."

"December 14

"What is this, my dear friend? I'm frightened by myself! Is not
my love for her the holiest, purest, most brotherly love? Have I
ever felt a culpable desire in my heart? —I will not protest—And
now, dreams! Oh, how right those people were who ascribed these
contradictory effects to alien powers. Last night, I tremble to say it,
I held her in my arms, pressed her close to my breast, and covered
her lips, which whispered love to me, with countless kisses; my eyes
swam in the intoxication of hers! Heaven! am I culpable for feeling
bliss even now, when I recall these ardent joys in all their depth?
Lotte, Lotte! —It's all over with me! My senses are becoming con-

---

1. Werther is here addressing himself.

fused, for a week I have been without reflective power. My eyes are filled with tears, I feel happy nowhere and everywhere. I desire nothing and ask for nothing. It would be better for me if I went."

The resolve to leave the world had at this time, under these circumstances, gained more and more power over Werther's mind. Since his return to Lotte it had always been his ultimate prospect and hope; but he had told himself that it must not be a hasty, rash deed; he would take this step with the firmest conviction, with the utmost resolution possible.

His doubts and his inner conflict are revealed by a note which is probably the beginning of a letter to Wilhelm and which was found, undated, among his papers:

"Her presence, her fate, her sympathy with mine press the last tears from my burning brain.

"To lift the curtain and step behind it, that is everything. And why this hesitation and delay? Because we do not know what things look like behind it, and because one cannot return, and because it is a characteristic of our mind to suspect confusion and darkness where we know nothing definite."

He finally became more and more familiar and friendly with the mournful thought, and his resolution became firm and irrevocable, to which the following ambiguous letter, written to his friend, bears testimony.

"December 20

"I owe it to your love, Wilhelm, that you have taken my words in this spirit. Yes, you are right: it would be better for me if I went. Your proposal that I should return to you is not altogether to my liking; at least I should like to make a detour first, especially as we may expect a lasting frost and good roads. I am also very happy to know that you are willing to come and fetch me; only put it off for another fortnight and wait for one more letter from me with further news. Nothing must be plucked before it is ripe. And a fortnight more or less may make a great difference. Tell my mother to pray for her son and that I beg her forgiveness for all the distress I have caused her. It was simply my destiny to sadden those to whom I owed joy. Farewell, my dearest friend! All the blessings of Heaven upon you. Farewell!"

What was going on in Lotte's mind during this time, her attitude toward her husband and her unhappy friend, we scarcely dare express in words, although we can form our own ideas of it from our knowledge of her character, and a refined feminine soul[2] can appreciate her thoughts and feelings.

This much is certain: she was firmly resolved in her own mind to do her utmost to send Werther away, and if she hesitated, it was out of a warm, friendly desire to spare him, because she knew how hard, in fact almost impossible, it would be, for him to go. However, at this time she was pressed harder to take serious action; her husband was completely silent about the relationship, as she, too, had always kept silent about it, and she was all the more anxious to prove to him by her actions that her attitude was worthy of his.

On the same day on which Werther had written the above letter to his friend—it was the Sunday before Christmas—he came to Lotte in the evening and found her alone. She was busy finishing some toys which she had constructed as a Christmas gift for her brothers and sisters. He talked of the joy the children would feel and of the time of life when the unexpected opening of the door and the sight of a decorated tree with wax candles, candy, and apples transported a child into a heavenly ecstasy. —"You, too," said Lotte, concealing her embarrassment behind a sweet smile, "you, too, will get a gift if you are really nice; a little roll of wax tapers and something else." "And what do you call being nice?" he exclaimed. "How do you expect me to be, how can I be, dearest Lotte?" —"Thursday evening is Christmas Eve," she said. "The children will come and father too, and everyone will get his gift. You may come too—but not before then." —Werther was taken aback. —"Please," she continued, "it must be so, I beg of you for the sake of my peace of mind, things cannot, cannot go on this way." —He averted his gaze from her, walked up and down the room muttering between his teeth, "Things cannot go on this way."

Lotte, who sensed the terrible state into which these words had plunged him, sought to divert his thoughts by all sorts of questions, but in vain. —"No, Lotte!" he exclaimed, "I shall not see you again!" "Why so?" she replied, "Werther, you can, you must see us again, but control yourself. Oh, why did you have to be born with this vehemence, this unconquerable, clinging passion for everything you touch? I beg you," she continued, taking him by the hand, "control yourself. Your intelligence, your knowledge, your

2. *Schöne Seele*, a popular phrase of the period, used also by Rousseau (*belle âme*). It denoted a person who enjoys a natural harmony between his intellect and instincts, between duty and desires. With its roots in Plato and Plotinus, the conception was given classic formulation by Schiller in his essay *Über Anmut und Würde* (1793) and by Goethe in the sixth book of *Wilhelm Meisters Lehrjahre* (1795).

talents, what a variety of delights they offer you! Be a man! Remove this melancholy attachment from a person who can do nothing but feel sorry for you." He ground his teeth and looked at her gloomily. She held his hand. "Calm your mind just for one moment, Werther," she said. "Don't you feel that you are deceiving yourself, deliberately destroying yourself? Why must you love me, Werther? Why just me, who belong to another man? Why just this? I fear, I fear, it is only the impossibility of possessing me that makes your desire for me so strong." —He withdrew his hand from hers, and looked at her with a fixed, angry stare. —"Smart!" he cried, "very smart! Did Albert possibly make this remark? Diplomatic! Very diplomatic!" "Anyone might say it," she replied. "And is there no girl in the whole world who could fulfill your heart's desire? Exert your will power to look for her, and I swear to you that you will find her; both for your sake and ours I have been unhappy with the way you have lately confined yourself within this circumscribed sphere. Exert your will power! A journey will, must distract you. Seek and find an object worthy of your love, and then return and let us enjoy together the happiness of a true friendship."

"This could be printed," he said with a cold laugh, "and recommended to every schoolmaster. Dear Lotte, give me a little more peace and everything will come out right." —"Only one thing, Werther, do not come back before Christmas Eve." —He was about to reply, but Albert came into the room. They bade each other a frosty good evening and paced up and down the room side by side in embarrassment. Werther began a trivial conversation, which soon came to an end. Albert did the same, and then asked his wife about certain domestic matters; when he heard that they had not been attended to yet, he said a few words to her which seemed cold, even harsh to Werther. He wanted to go but could not, and delayed till eight o'clock, his displeasure and irritability growing all the time, until the table was set and he took his hat and cane. Albert invited him to stay, but Werther, thinking he heard only meaningless polite words, thanked him coldly and left.

He returned home, took the candle from the hand of his servant, who wanted to light the way for him, and went to his room alone. He wept aloud, talked excitedly to himself, walked up and down the room vehemently, and finally threw himself fully dressed on the bed, where the srvant found him when he dared to go in at about eleven o'clock to ask if he should take his master's boots off. Werther permitted it and forbade the servant to enter the room the next morning before he was summoned.

On Monday morning, the twenty-first of December, he wrote the following letter to Lotte, which was found, sealed, on his desk after his death and was delivered to her. I shall insert it here in instalments, just as, to judge by the circumstances, he seems to have written it.

"My mind is made up, Lotte, I want to die. I am writing this to you without romantic extravagance, calmly, on the morning of the day on which I shall see you for the last time. When you read this, my dearest one, the cool grave will already cover the stiff remains of the restless, unhappy man who knows of no sweeter delight in the last moments of his life than to converse with you. I have had a frightful night, and ah! a beneficent night. It is this night which has confirmed and fixed my resolution: I want to die! When I tore myself from you yesterday, in the fearful rebellion of my senses, when everything pressed toward my heart, and my hopeless, joylesss existence near you gripped me with a gruesome coldness—I was scarcely able to reach my room; I threw myself on my knees, beside myself, and You, God, did grant me the final comfort of the bitterest tears! A thousand plans, a thousand prospects raged in my soul, and finally it stood there, firm, whole, the ultimate and sole thought: I want to die! —I lay down, and in the morning, in the calm of awakening, it still stands firm, still strong in my heart: I want to die! —It is not despair, it is the certainty that I have reached the end of my suffering³ and that I am sacrificing myself for you. Yes, Lotte! Why should I conceal it? One of us three must go, and I am willing to be that one. Oh, my dearest one! In this torn heart the frenzied thought has prowled about, often—to murder your husband—you—myself!—So be it then. —When you climb the mountain on a beautiful summer evening, remember me, how I often came up the valley; and then look over toward the churchyard at my grave, see how the wind makes the tall grass sway back and forth in the light of the setting sun. —I was calm when I began, but now, when all this becomes so vivid to me, I weep like a child."—

Toward ten o'clock Werther called his servant and, while dressing, told him that he was going on a journey in a few days; he was, therefore, to take out his clothes and prepare everything for packing. He also ordered him to call in all his bills, get back some books he had lent, and pay some poor people, to whom he usually gave a weekly allowance, their allotted share for two months in advance.

3. The German text has *ausgetragen*, which means bearing a child the full nine months of pregnancy. So Werther has reached his time.

He had his meal brought to his room and, after eating it, rode out to visit the magistrate, whom he did not find at home. He walked up and down the garden deep in thought, as if, in the end, he wished to heap on himself the full measure of melancholy memories.

The children did not leave him in peace for long; they pursued him, jumped on him, told him that after tomorrow and another tomorrow and one more day they would get their Christmas gifts from Lotte; and they told him all the wonderful things they pictured in their childish imaginations. —"Tomorrow!" he exclaimed, "and another tomorrow, and one more day"—and kissed them all warmly and was about to leave them when the little fellow wanted to whisper something in his ear. He confided to him that his big brothers had written beautiful New Year's greetings, So Big! and one for papa, one for Albert and Lotte, and one for Herr Werther too; they were going to present them early on New Year's Day. This overwhelmed him. He gave something to each of them, mounted his horse, left regards for the old gentleman, and rode off with tears in his eyes.

He arrived home at about five o'clock, gave orders to the maid to attend to the fire to keep it going into the night. He told his servant to pack books and linen into the bottom of the trunk, and to sew his clothes up in a bundle. Then he probably wrote the following paragraph of his last letter to Lotte:

"You are not expecting me. You think I will obey you and not see you before Christmas Eve. O Lotte! It's today or never. On Christmas Eve you will hold this paper in your hand, you will tremble and moisten it with your precious tears. I will, I must! Oh, how happy I feel in my resolution."

Lotte had meanwhile fallen into a peculiar mental state. After her last conversation with Werther she had felt how difficult it would be for her to part from him, how much he would suffer if he left her.

It had been mentioned in Albert's presence, as though in passing, that Werther would not come again before Christmas Eve, and Albert had gone on horseback to see an official in the district with whom he had some business to transact and where he was to stay overnight.

She now sat alone; none of her brothers or sisters was with her, and she abandoned herself to her thoughts, which silently revolved about her situation. She now saw herself tied forever to the man whose love and loyalty were familiar to her, to whom she was devoted with all her heart, whose tranquility and trustworthiness really seemed destined by Heaven to serve as the basis for a good woman's lifelong happiness; she felt what he would always be to her and to their children. On the other hand, Werther had become very dear to her; from the first moment of their acquaintance the harmony of their minds had turned out to be so beautiful, her long and continuous association with him, the many situations they had experienced together had made an indelible impression on her heart. Every thing of interest that she felt and thought, she was accustomed to share with him, and his departure threatened to open a gap in her entire existence which could never be filled. Oh, if at that moment she could have transformed him into a brother, how happy she would have been! —If she could have married him off to one of her friends, if she could have hoped that his relationship with Albert might be completely restored to its former state.

She had thought of her friends one by one, but saw something to object to in every one of them and found none to whom she would gladly have yielded him.

Amid all these reflections she felt deeply for the first time, without realizing it clearly, that the secret longing of her heart was to keep him for herself, but she also told herself that she could not, must not, keep him; her pure, beautiful nature, usually so light and so ready to solve difficulties, felt the oppressive melancholy to which the prospect of happiness is closed. Her heart was heavy, and a cloud of gloom hung over her eyes.

It was half past six when she heard Werther coming up the stairs, and she soon recognized his step and his voice, which asked for her. How her heart pounded at his approach—one might almost say for the first time. She would have liked to deny him her presence, and when he came in she cried out to him with a sort of passionate confusion· "You have not kept your word." —"I promised nothing," was his reply. —"Then you should at least have granted my wish," she replied, "I begged you for peace of mind for us both."

She did not quite know what she was saying, any more than what she was doing, when she sent out for some friends, so that she would not have to be alone with Werther. He put down some books which he had brought, asked about others, and she wished at one moment that her friends would come, the next that they would not. The maid came back and reported that they both sent their regrets.

She wanted to have the maid sit in the next room over her sewing; then she changed her mind. Werther paced up and down the room, and she went to the piano and began to play a minuet, but it refused to come smoothly. She composed herself and sat down calmly beside Werther, who had taken his usual place on the sofa.

"Have you nothing to read?" she said. —He had nothing. —"There in my drawer," she said, "is your translation[4] of some songs of Ossian; I haven't read them yet, for I kept hoping to hear them from you; but since then I have never been able to find or make the opportunity." —He smiled, fetched the songs; a shudder went through him as he took them in his hands, and his eyes filled with tears as he looked at them. He sat down and read:

Star[5] of descending night! fair is thy light in the west! thou liftest thy unshorn head from thy cloud; thy steps are stately on thy hill. What dost thou behold in the plain? The stormy winds are laid. The murmur of the torrent comes from afar. Roaring waves climb the distant rock. The flies of evening are on their feeble wings; the hum of their course is on the field. What dost thou behold, fair light? But thou dost smile and depart. Thy waves come with joy around thee: they bathe thy lovely hair. Farewell, thou silent beam- Let the light of Ossian's soul arise!

And it does arise in its strength! I behold my departed friends. Their gathering is on Lora, as in the days of other years. Fingal comes like a watery column of mist; his heroes are around. And see the bards of song, grey-haired Ullin! stately Ryno! Alpin, with the tuneful voice! the soft complaint of Minona! How are ye changed, my friends, since the days of Selma's feast? when we contended like gales of spring, as they fly along the hill, and bend by turns the feebly-whistling grass.

Minona came forth in her beauty; with downcast look and tearful eye. Her hair flew slowly on the blast that rushed unfrequent from the hill. The souls of the heroes were sad when she raised the tuneful voice. Often had they seen the grave of Salgar, the dark dwelling of white-bosomed Colma. Colma left alone on the hill, with all her voice of song!

4. Goethe's. The passage which follows is from *Songs of Selma*, one of the shorter poems of Macpherson-Ossian. Goethe translated it in Strassburg during his first enthusiasm for Ossian; the version printed in the German text was made especially for *Werther*. It departs considerably from Macpherson's text, which is given in its original form.

5. The situation presented in the passage is rather complex. The hoary bard Ossian sings a song to the evening star (page 84, lines 12–19). He then recalls the feast of Selma, held at Lora, the royal hall of his father Fingal, King of the Caledonians, on the northwestern coast of Scotland. Ossian then sings three songs which he once heard at Selma's feast. The first of these was sung by Minona; its theme is the lament of Colma, who waited in vain for the appearance of her lover Salgar, who did not come to her because he and Colmar's brother had killed each other (page 85, line 3, to page 86, line 1). The second song is sung by the bard Ullin. Its theme is the death of Minona's brother Morar; in form it is a dialogue between Ryno and Alpin. In Ullin's recitation the role of Alpin was sung by Ullin, that of Ryno by Ossian himself (page 86, line 5). The third song is sung by Armin, who laments the death of his children. His daughter Dama had been abducted and taken overseas by Erath, who was captured by her brother Arindal. Dama's lover, Armar, mistakes Arindal for the abductor Erath and kills him. He then leaps into the water to rescue Dama but is drowned. Dama dies on a rock from grief, in view of her father Armin (page 86, line 47, to page 88, line 6.) Goethe has used virtually the whole poem, omitting only the last paragraph.

Salgar promised to come: but the night descended around. Hear the voice of Colma, when she sat alone on the hill!

Colma

It is night; I am alone, forlorn on the hill of storms. The wind is heard in the mountain. The torrent pours down the rock. No hut receives me from the rain, forlorn on the hill of winds.

Rise, moon! from behind thy clouds. Stars of the night, arise! Lead me, some light, to the place where my love rests from the chase alone! his bow near him, unstrung: his dogs panting around him. But here I must sit alone, by the rock of the mossy stream. The stream and the wind roar aloud. I hear not the voice of my love!

Why delays my Salgar, why the chief of the hill, his promise? Here is the rock, and here the tree! here is the roaring stream! Thou didst promise with night to be here. Ah! whither is my Salgar gone? With thee I would fly from my father; with thee, from my brother of pride. Our race have long been foes; we are not foes, O Salgar!

Cease a little while, O wind! stream, be thou silent a while! let my voice be heard around. Let my wanderer hear me! Salgar! it is Colma who calls. Here is the tree, and the rock. Salgar, my love! I am here. Why delayest thou thy coming?

Lo! the calm moon comes forth. The flood is bright in the vale. The rocks are gray on the steep. I see him not on the brow. His dogs come not before him, with tidings of his near approach. Here I must sit alone!

Who lie on the heath beside me? Are they my love and my brother? Speak to me, O my friends! To Colma they give no reply. Speak to me: I am alone! My soul is tormented with fears! Ah, they are dead! Their swords are red from the fight. O my brother! my brother! why. hast thou slain my Salgar? why, O Salgar! hast thou slain my brother? Dear were ye both to me! what shall I say in your praise? Thou wert fair on the hill among thousands! he was terrible in fight. Speak to me; hear my voice; hear me, sons of my love! They are silent; silent for ever! Cold, cold are their breasts of clay!

Oh! from the rock on the hill; from the top of the windy steep, speak, ye ghosts of the dead! speak, I will not be afraid! Whither are ye gone to rest? In what cave of the hill shall I find the departed? No feeble voice is on the gale; no answer half-drowned in the storm!

I sit in my grief! I wait for morning in my tears! Rear the tomb, ye friends of the dead. Close it not till Colma come. My life flies away like a dream! why should I stay behind? Here shall I rest with my friends, by the stream of the sounding rock. When night comes on the hill; when the loud winds arise; my ghost shall stand in the blast, and mourn the death of my friends. The hunter shall hear from his booth. He shall fear, but love my voice! For sweet shall my voice be for my friends: pleasant were her friends to Colma!

Such was thy song, Minona, softly-blushing daughter of Torman. Our tears descended from Colma, and our souls were sad!

Ullin came with his harp; he gave the song of Alpin. The voice of Alpin was pleasant; the soul of Ryno was a beam of fire! But they had rested in the narrow house: their voice had ceased in Selma. Ullin had returned, one day, from the chase, before the heroes fell. He heard their strife on the hill; their song was soft but sad. They mourned the fall of Morar, first of mortal men! His soul was like the soul of Fingal; his sword like the sword of Oscar.[6] But he fell, and his father mourned: his sister's eyes were full of tears. Minona's eyes were full of tears, the sister of car-borne Morar. She retired from the song of Ullin, like the moon in the west, when she foresees the shower, and hides her fair head in a cloud. I touched the harp, with Ullin; the song of mourning rose!

Ryno

The wind and the rain are past: calm is the noon of day. The clouds are divided in heaven. Over the green hills flies the inconstant sun. Red through the stony vale comes down the stream of the hill. Sweet are thy murmurs, O stream! but more sweet is the voice I hear. It is the voice of Alpin, the son of song, mourning for the dead! Bent is his head of age; red his tearful eye. Alpin, thou son of song, why alone on the silent hill? why complainest thou, as a blast in the woods; as a wave on the lonely shore?

Alpin

My tears, O Ryno! are for the dead; my voice for those that have passed away. Tall thou art on the hill; fair among the sons of the vale. But thou shalt fall like Morar; the mourner shall sit on thy tomb. The hill shall know thee no more; thy bow shall lie in thy hall unstrung!

Thou wert swift, O Morar! as a roe on the desert; terrible as a meteor of fire. Thy wrath was as the storm. Thy sword in battle, as lightning in the field. Thy voice was a stream after rain; like thunder on distant hills. Many fell by thy arm; they were consumed in the flames of thy wrath. But when thou didst return from the war, how peaceful was thy brow! Thy face was like the sun after rain; like the moon in the silence of night; calm as the breast of the lake when the loud wind is laid.

Narrow is thy dwelling now! dark the place of thine abode! With three steps I compass thy grave, O thou who wast so great before! Four stones, with their heads of moss are the only memorial of thee. A tree with scarce a leaf, long grass which whistles in the wind, mark to the hunter's eye the grave of the mighty Morar. Morar! thou art low indeed. Thou hast no mother to mourn thee; no maid with her tears of love. Dead is she that brought thee forth. Fallen is the daughter of Morglan.

Who on his staff is this? who is this, whose head is white with age? whose eyes are red with tears? who quakes at every step? It is thy father, O Morar! the father of no son but thee. He heard of thy fame in war; he heard of foes dispersed. He heard of Morar's renown; why did he not hear of his wound? Weep, thou father of Morar! weep; but thy son heareth thee not. Deep is the sleep of the dead; low their pillow of dust. No more shall he hear thy voice; no more awake at thy call. When shall it be morn in the grave, to bid the slumberer awake?

Farewell, thou bravest of men! thou conqueror in the field! but the field shall see thee no more; nor the dark wood be lightened with the splendor of thy steel. Thou hast left no son. The song shall preserve thy name. Future times shall hear of thee; they shall hear of the fallen Morar!

The grief of all arose, but most the bursting sigh of Armin. He remembers the death of his son, who fell in the days of his youth.

6. Oscar, the son of Ossian; he figures in many of the Ossianic poems.

Carmor was near the hero, the chief of the echoing Galmal. "Why bursts the sigh of Armin?" he said. "Is there a cause to mourn? The song comes, with its music, to melt and please the soul. It is like soft mist that, rising from a lake, pours on the silent vale; the green flowers are filled with dew, but the sun returns in his strength, and the mist is gone. Why art thou sad, O Armin! chief of sea-surrounded Gorma?"

"Sad I am! nor small is my cause of woe! Carmor, thou hast lost no son; thou hast lost no daughter of beauty. Colgar the valiant lives; and Annira, fairest maid. The boughs of thy house ascend, O Carmor! but Armin is the last of his race. Dark is thy bed, O Daura! deep thy sleep in the tomb! When shalt thou awake with thy songs? with all thy voice of music?

"Arise, winds of Autumn, arise; blow along the heath! streams of the mountains, roar! roar, tempests, in the groves of my oaks! walk through broken clouds, O moon! show thy pale face, at intervals! bring to my mind the night, when all my children fell; when Arindal the mighty fell; when Daura the lovely failed!

"Daura, my daughter! thou wert fair; fair as the moon on Fura; white as the driven snow; sweet as the breathing gale. Arindal, thy bow was strong. Thy spear was swift in the field. Thy look was like mist on the wave; thy shield, a red cloud in a storm.

"Armar, renowned in war, came, and sought Daura's love. He was not long refused: fair was the hope of their friends!

"Erath, son of Odgal, repined; his brother had been slain by Armar. He came disguised like a son of the sea: fair was his skiff on the wave; white his locks of age; calm his serious brow. 'Fairest of women,' he said, 'lovely daughter of Armin! a rock not distant in the sea bears a tree on its side; red shines the fruit afar. There Armar waits for Daura. I come to carry his love!'

"She went; she called on Armar. Nought answered, but the son of the rock, 'Armar, my love! my love! why tormentest thou me with fear? Hear, son of Arnart, hear: it is Daura who calleth thee!'

"Erath the traitor fled laughing to the land. She lifted up her voice; she called for her brother and her father. 'Arindal! Armin! none to relieve your Daura!'

"Her voice came over the sea. Arindal my son descended from the hill; rough in the spoils of the chase. His arrows rattled by his side; his bow was in his hand: five dark gray dogs attend his steps. He saw fierce Erath on the shore: he seized and bound him to an oak. Thick wind the thongs of the hide around his limbs; he loads the wind with his groans.

"Arindal ascends the deep in his boat, to bring Daura to land. Armar came in his wrath, and let fly the grey-feathered shaft. It sung; it sunk in thy heart, O Arindal, my son! for Erath the traitor thou diedst. The oar is stopped at once; he panted on the rock and expired. What is thy grief, O Daura, when round thy feet is poured thy brother's blood!

"The boat is broken in twain. Armar plunges into the sea, to rescue his Daura, or die. Sudden a blast from the hill came over the waves. He sank and he rose no more.

"Alone, on the sea-beat rock, my daughter was heard to complain. Frequent and loud were her cries. What could her father do? All night I stood on the shore. I saw her by the faint beam of the moon. All night I heard her cries. Loud was the wind; the rain beat hard on the hill. Before morning appeared her voice was weak. It died away, like the evening-breeze among the grass of the rocks. Spent with grief she expired; and left thee, Armin, alone. Gone is my strength in war! fallen my pride among women![7]

"When the storms aloft arise; when the north lifts the wave on high; I sit by the sounding shore, and look on the fatal rock. Often by the setting moon, I see the ghosts of my children. Half viewless, they walk in mournful conference together."

A flood of tears that streamed from Lotte's eyes and relieved her burdened heart checked Werther's recitation. He threw the papers down, grasped her hand and wept the bitterest tears. Lotte supported herself on the other hand and covered her eyes with her handkerchief. Both manifested a fearful agitation. They felt their own misery in the destiny of the heroes, felt it together and were united in their tears. Werther's lips and eyes burned on Lotte's arms; a shudder possessed her and she wanted to withdraw; pain and sympathy lay upon her like a leaden weight, numbing her senses. She took a deep breath, hoping to compose herself, and, sobbing, begged him to continue, begged him with the full voice of heaven. Werther trembled and, his heart ready to burst, picked up the sheets and read in a broken voice:

Why dost thou awake me, O breath of spring, thou dost woo me and say, "I cover thee with the drops of heaven."[8] But the time of my fading is near, the blast that shall scatter my leaves. Tomorrow shall the traveler come; he that saw me in my beauty shall come. His eyes will search the field, but they will not find me.—

The full force of these words descended on the unhappy man. He threw himself down before Lotte in all his despair, grasped her hands, pressed them to his eyes, against his forehead, and a premonition of his terrible resolve seemed to rush through her mind. Her senses became confused, she pressed his hands, pressed them against her breast, leaned toward him with a mournful movement, and their glowing cheeks touched. The world ceased to exist for them. He threw his arms about her, pressed her to his breast, and covered her trembling, stammering lips with violent kisses. —"Werther!" she cried in a suffocating voice, turning from him, "Werther!" and with a weak hand she pushed his body away from hers. "Werther!" she cried in the steady tone of the noblest emotion. —He did not resist, released her from his arms and threw himself before her, senseless. She jumped up, and in confusion and anxiety, quivering between love and anger, she said, "This is the last time, Werther. You shall not see me again." —And, casting a look full of love at the wretched man, she hurried into the next room and locked the

<hr>

7. Strength . . . pride, i.e., his son and daughter, respectively.

8. This passage is from a different poem of Macpherson, *Berrathon*. It concentrates into a few lines the motif of death which now haunts Werther.

door behind her. Werther extended his arms after her but did not dare to retain her. He lay on the floor, his head on the sofa, and remained in this position for more than half an hour, until a noise brought him back to his senses. It was the maid, who wanted to set the table. He paced up and down the room, and when he found himself alone again, he went to the door of the study and called in a low voice: "Lotte! Lotte! just one more word, a word of farewell." —She was silent. He waited and begged and waited; then he tore himself away and cried: "Farewell, Lotte! Farewell forever!"

He came to the city gate. The guards, who knew him, let him out without a word. A mixture of rain and snow was falling, and he did not knock at the door again till about eleven. His servant noticed that his master was without his hat when he came home. He did not venture to say anything, he helped him undress; all his clothes were wet. Later, his hat was found on a rock which overhangs the valley from the slope of the hill; it is beyond comprehension how he could have climbed this rock on a dark, wet night without falling.

He went to bed and slept long. Next morning, when he answered Werther's call and brought him his coffee, the servant found him writing. He added the following to his letter to Lotte:

"For the last time, then, for the last time I open these eyes. They shall, alas, never see the sun again, for a gloomy, foggy day obscures it. Mourn then, O Nature! Your son, your friend, your lover is approaching his end. Lotte, this is an incomparable feeling, and yet it comes closest to a twilight dream to say to yourself: this is the last morning. The last! Lotte, I have no feeling for that word: last. Do I not stand here in all my strength, and tomorrow I shall lie on the ground, stretched out and limp? To die: what does that mean? Behold, we dream when we talk of death. I have seen many die; but so restricted is human nature that it has no feeling for the beginning or end of its existence. At this moment there is still mine and yours—yours, O my beloved. And in another moment—separated, parted—perhaps forever? —No, Lotte, no—How can I pass away? How can you pass away? For we exist! —Pass away—what does that mean? It is just another word, an empty sound, which does not touch my heart. —Dead, Lotte! buried in the cold ground, so confined, so dark! —I had a friend[9] who was everything to me in my helpless youth; she died and I followed her corpse and stood at her grave when they lowered the coffin and then pulled the whirring ropes from under it and up again; then the first shovelful of earth pattered down, and the

9. See page 5.

frightened box reverberated with a dull thud which grew duller and duller until at last it was completely covered. —I threw myself down beside the grave—moved, shaken, frightened, ravaged to the core; but I did not know what was happening to me—what will happen to me—Dying! Grave! I don't understand these words.

"Oh forgive me, forgive me! Yesterday! It should have been the last moment of my life. Oh you angel! For the first time, for the first time without any doubt whatever, the joyful feeling glows through my innermost depths: she loves me! she loves me! The sacred fire that streamed from your lips is still burning on mine; a new, warm joy is in my heart. Forgive me! Forgive me!

"Oh, I knew that you loved me, knew it from the first soulful looks, from the first handclasp, and yet, when I was away from you, when I saw Albert at your side, I despaired again in feverish doubt.

"Do you remember the flowers you sent me when you could not say a word to me at that awful party and could not give me your hand? Oh, I knelt before them through half the night, and they put the seal on your love for me. But alas, these impressions passed, as the soul of the believer gradually loses the feeling of grace given him by his God with all the fullness of Heaven, with a sacred, visible symbol.

"All this is transitory, but no eternity shall extinguish the glowing life which I savored yesterday on your lips, and which I feel within me now. She loves me! This arm has embraced her, these lips have trembled on hers, this mouth has stammered words on hers. She is mine! You are mine! Yes, Lotte, forever.

"And what does it signify that Albert is your husband? Husband! That is something for this world—and for this world it is a sin that I love you, that I should like to snatch you out of his arms into mine. Sin? Very well! And I am punishing myself for it; I have tasted this sin in all its heavenly rapture, I have sucked the balm of life and strength into my heart. From this moment on you are mine. Mine, Lotte! I am going ahead, going to my Father, to your Father. I will bring my plaint to Him and He will comfort me until you come, and I will fly to meet you, clasp you, and remain with you before the countenance of the Infinite in an eternal embrace.

"I am not dreaming, I am not delusional; so near the grave the light grows brighter for me. We shall be![1] We shall see each other again! To see your mother! I shall see her, shall find her, ah, and pour out my whole heart to her! Your mother, your image."

Toward eleven o'clock Werther asked his servant whether Albert

1. Werther refers to Lotte's words on page 42, line 13.

had returned yet. The servant replied: yes, he had seen his horse being led home. Thereupon his master gave him an unsealed note with the following content:

"Will you loan me your pistols for a journey I am planning? Farewell."

The dear woman had slept little that night; what she had feared had been realized in a way she could neither have suspected nor dreaded. Her blood, which usually flowed so pure and light, was in a feverish rebellion; a thousand different emotions ravaged her fair heart. Was it the fire of Werther's embraces she felt in her bosom? Was it displeasure at his boldness? Was it an irritating comparison between her present state and the days of perfectly natural, naive innocence and carefree confidence in herself? How was she to face her husband? How confess to him a scene that she might well confess but which she nevertheless did not dare confess? They had been silent toward each other for such a long time[2]; was she to be the first to break the silence and make such an unexpected revelation to her husband at this inopportune time? She was afraid that the mere report of Werther's visit would make an unpleasant impression on him, how much more this unexpected catastrophe! Could she really hope that her husband would see it in its true light and accept it entirely without prejudice? Dare she wish that he might read her soul? But then again, could she dissimulate before the man toward whom she had always been open and free like glass of clear crystal, and from whom she never had, nor could have, concealed any of her feelings? Either alternative was a cause of anxiety and embarrassment to her; and always her thoughts returned to Werther, who was lost to her, whom she could not give up, yet whom she must unfortunately abandon to himself and for whom there was nothing left when he had lost her.

At that moment she could not clearly understand how heavily the estrangement that had settled over them now weighed on her. Such intelligent, such good people began to observe a silence toward each other because of certain private differences, each pondering his right and the other's wrong, and the relationship grew so entangled and so harassed that it became impossible to loosen the knot at the critical moment on which everything depended. If a happy intimacy had re-established their former closeness sooner, if their mutual love and understanding had flourished and opened their hearts, perhaps there might still have been help for our friend.

Another strange circumstance entered the situation. Werther, as

---

2. This contradiction to the statement on page 76, line 4, results from additions which Goethe made in the second version of *Werther*.

we know from his letters, had never made a secret of the fact that he longed to leave this world. Albert had often challenged him on it; Lotte and her husband had sometimes discussed the subject too. Albert, who felt a decided aversion to the act, had quite often, with a sort of irritation that was wholly out of character, made it very clear that he had reason to doubt the seriousness of such an intention; he had even permitted himself to joke about the matter and had communicated his skepticism to Lotte. This, to be sure, calmed her when her thoughts presented the sad picture to her; on the other hand, it made her feel reluctant to inform her husband of the anxiety that tormented her at the moment.

Albert returned and Lotte went to meet him with an embarrassed haste. He was not in a cheerful mood; his business had not been completed and he had found in the neighboring magistrate a petty, unbending man. The bad road, too, had spoiled his temper.

He asked whether anything had happened, and she answered with excessive haste that Werther had been there the night before. He asked if any letters had come and received the reply that a letter and some packages were lying in his room. He went in and Lotte remained alone. The presence of the man whom she loved and honored had made a new impression on her heart. The memory of his noble spirit, his love, and kindness had somewhat calmed her emotions, and she felt a secret impulse to follow him; she took her sewing and went into his room, as she was accustomed to do. She found him occupied opening his packages and reading. Some of the contents did not seem to be of the most agreeable sort. She put some questions to him, which he answered curtly, and then took up his position at his desk to write.

They had been together like this for an hour and Lotte's heart was sinking lower and lower. She felt how difficult it would be for her to reveal to her husband what weighed on her mind, even if he were in the best of humors; she lapsed into a state of melancholy, which became all the more frightening to her as she sought to conceal it and to choke back her tears.

The appearance of Werther's servant threw her into the greatest embarrassment. He handed the note to Albert, who turned calmly to his wife and said: "Give him the pistols." —"I wish him a happy journey," he said to the boy. The words struck her like a thunderclap; she staggered to her feet, not knowing what she was doing. Slowly she went to the wall; she trembled as she took down the weapons, dusted them off, and hesitated, and she would have hesitated longer still if Albert had not pressed her with a questioning look. She handed the boy the dreadful weapons without being able to utter a word, and when the boy had left the house she gathered up her work and went to her room in a state of the most indescribable uncertainty. Her heart foretold her every possible terror. At one point she was on the verge of throwing herself at the feet of her husband, and disclosing everything to him: the events of the previous evening, her guilt, and her forebodings. Then, again, she saw no solution in such a course of action, least of all could she hope to persuade her husband to go to Werther. The table was set; a good friend, who had merely come in to ask a question, and intended to go at once but stayed on, made the dinner conversation endurable. They forced themselves to talk, told stories and forgot themselves.

The boy brought the pistols to Werther, who took them from him with delight when he heard that Lotte had handed them to him. He had bread and wine[3] brought up, told the boy to have his dinner, and sat down to write:

"They have passed through your hands, you dusted them off; I kiss them a thousand times, for you have touched them. And you, heavenly spirit, favor my resolve! And you, Lotte, hand me the instrument, you, from whose hands I wished to receive death, and, ah, receive it now. Oh, I questioned my boy. You trembled when you handed them to him, you did not say farewell. —Alas, alas, no farewell! —Can you have closed your heart to me for the sake of the moment which bound me to you forever? Lotte, not even a thousand years can efface the impression! and I feel it: you cannot hate the man who burns so passionately for you."

After dinner he ordered the boy to finish packing, tore up many papers, and went out to take care of some small debts. He came home again, then went out once more, through the town gate, heedless of the rain, into the Count's garden, wandered about in the area, returned home as night descended, and wrote:

"Wilhelm, I have seen the fields and the woods and the sky for the last time. Farewell to you, too! Dear mother, forgive me. Comfort her, Wilhelm. God bless you both. All my affairs are in order. Farewell! We shall see each other again, in happier circumstances."

"I have ill rewarded you, Albert, but you will forgive me. I have disturbed the peace of your home, I have brought distrust between

---

3. Possibly an allusion to the Last Supper, in line with Werther's version of himself as a Christlike martyr.

you. Farewell; I will end it. Oh I pray that my death may restore your happiness. Albert, Albert, make the angel happy! And so may God's blessing be upon you."

That evening he continued to rummage among his papers, tore up many and threw them into the stove, and sealed some packages addressed to Wilhelm. They contained short essays and fragmentary thoughts, some of which I have seen. At ten o'clock he had the fire replenished and a bottle of wine brought in. He then sent his servant to bed, whose bedroom, like those of the other servants, was far to the rear of the house. The boy slept in his clothes so that he could be at hand early next morning; for his master had told him that the post horses would be in front of the house before six.

"After 11 o'clock

"Everything is so silent around me and my soul is calm too. I thank You, Lord, for giving me such warmth, such strength, in these last moments.

"I go to the window, my dearest one, and I can still see individual stars in the eternal sky, through the passing storm clouds. No, you will not fall! The Eternal One bears you on His heart and me too. I see the handle of the Great Wain, which I love best of all the constellations. When I went from you at night, as I left your gate, it stood facing me. With what intoxication have I often looked at it! Often, with uplifted hands, I have made it the symbol, the sacred milestone of happiness I felt; and even now—O Lotte, doesn't everything remind me of you? Do you not surround me? And haven't I, like a child, greedily snatched up every trifle your sacred hands had touched?

"Beloved silhouette! I bequeath it back to you, Lotte, and beg you to revere it. I have pressed a thousand kisses on it, waved a thousand greetings to it when I went out or came home.

"I have asked your father in a note I sent him to protect my body. In the churchyard there are two linden trees, at the rear in the corner, toward the field; there I wish to rest. He can, he will do this for his friend. You ask him too. I do not expect God-fearing Christians to lay their bodies near that of a poor, unhappy man like me.[4] Ah, I wish you would bury me beside the road or in some lonely valley, so that priest and Levite[5] might pass the stone

---

4. Orthodox Christians refuse burial to a suicide in consecrated ground.

5. Allusion to Luke 10:31—33.

marker and bless themselves, and the Samaritan shed a tear.

"See, Lotte, I do not shudder to take into my hand the cold frightful cup, from which I shall drink the ecstasy of death. You handed it to me, and I do not hesitate. All! all the wishes and hopes of my life are thus fulfilled—to knock at the brazen portals of death, so cold, so stiff.

"If I could have experienced the joy of dying for you, Lotte, of sacrificing myself for you! I would die bravely, die joyfully, if I could restore to you the peace, the bliss of your life. But alas, it was granted only to a few noble souls to shed their blood for their dear ones and by their death to kindle a new life for their friends a hundredfold strong.

"I wish to be buried in these clothes, Lotte. You have touched them, hallowed them; I have requested this of your father too. My soul will hover over my coffin. My pockets are not to be emptied. This pale pink ribbon which you wore at your breast when I saw you for the first time among the children—O kiss them a thousand times and tell them about the fate of their unhappy friend. The dear creatures! They are crowding about me. Oh, how I clung to you! I could not leave you from the first moment. —This ribbon shall be buried with me. You gave it to me on my birthday. How eagerly I grasped it all. —Ah, I did not think that my road was to lead me to this. —Be calm, I beg you, be calm!—

"They are loaded—the clock strikes twelve. So be it then! Lotte, Lotte, farewell, farewell!"

A neighbor saw the flash of the powder and heard the report; but as it was followed by silence, he paid no attention to it.

At six in the morning the servant comes in with a light. He finds his master on the floor, the pistol, and blood. He cries to him, and touches him; no answer, only the death rattle. He runs for a doctor and for Albert. Lotte hears the bell and is seized with a trembling in all her limbs. She wakes her husband, they get up; the servant gives them the news, weeping and stuttering. Lotte sinks down unconscious at Albert's feet.

When the doctor came to the unhappy man, he found him on the floor beyond help, his pulse still beating but all his limbs paralyzed. He had shot himself through the head above the right eye; his brains were protruding. A vein was needlessly opened in his arm; the blood flowed, he was still breathing.

From the blood on the arm of the chair one could infer that he had done the deed as he sat before his desk, then slumped down in his chair thrashing about convulsively. He lay on his back near the window, exhausted, fully dressed, wearing his boots, his blue coat, and yellow vest.

The house, the neighbors, the whole town was in an uproar. Albert came in. Werther had been laid on the bed, his forehead bandaged; his face already touched with the look of death, he was unable to move a limb. A horrible rattle still came from his lungs, now weak, now stronger; the end was expected momentarily.

He had drunk only one glass of the wine. *Emilia Galotti*[6] lay open on his desk.

I shall say nothing of Albert's consternation nor of Lotte's grief.

The old magistrate, upon hearing the news, came galloping over; he kissed the dying man, shedding the most passionate tears. His oldest son soon followed after him on foot; they fell down beside the bed with an expression of the most uncontrollable anguish, and kissed his hands and lips; and the oldest, whom he had always liked best, clung to his lips until he had expired; and the boy was removed by force. He died at noon. The presence of the magistrate, and the measures he had taken, prevented a disturbance. At about eleven o'clock at night he had him buried at the spot which he had selected for himself. The old man and his sons followed the body; Albert was unable to do so. Lotte's life was feared to be in danger. Workmen bore him. No clergyman was present.[7]

6. See Afterword, p. 112.

7. Burial at night was usual in the eighteenth century; also that the coffin should be borne by the members of some guild. The absence of a clergyman at the burial is explained by the fact that in the eyes of the Church, Werther was a murderer. But it also underlines Werther's religious independence.

Johann Wolfgang von Goethe (1749-1832)

A Biographical Note

The events of Goethe's rich life are known to us in minute detail: his relationship to the men and women of his day, the books he read, the theaters he attended, the women he loved, the journeys he undertook. Goethe was a highly subjective artist. "All my writings are but fragments of a great confession," he said of himself. He regarded literature as a catharsis for the artist and as a vehicle for self-education. In his case, therefore, the examination of the life is not without relevance to an understanding of the work.[1]

Goethe was born in 1749 in Frankfurt am Main, of parents who were well-to-do and of some position in the community. His father was a nonpracticing lawyer, bearing the title of Imperial Councilor. Wolfgang was the oldest of six children, four of whom died in early childhood; only his sister Cornelia, one year younger than he, survived. He received his early schooling at home, with a strong emphasis on languages: Greek and Latin, English, French, Italian, Hebrew. He also took lessons in drawing and music (he played the piano and the flute). His first extant poem was written at the age of eight. On his thirteenth birthday he presented his father with a volume of his own poems.

He studied law, against his will, at the Universities of Leipzig (1765) and Strassburg (1770). At Strassburg he met Herder, the theologian and literary critic, who weaned the young student away from the neoclassical literary tradition in which he had been brought up and inspired him with enthusiasm for Homer, Pindar, Ossian, and Shakespeare, for folk poetry and Gothic architecture. Immediately, Goethe's poetry revealed the new spirit; it pulsates with a new vibrancy, freshness, naturalness, simplicity and is characterized by a bold break with the traditions imposed by grammar, syntax, and vocabulary.

After completing his law studies in 1771, Goethe settled in

1. See below, page 106.

Frankfurt, where he practiced law. However, he traveled frequently; several times he visited Darmstadt, Düsseldorf, and various other points in the Rhineland. He spent the summer of 1772 in Wetzlar, where he continued his legal education at the Imperial Chancery. In May he met Charlotte Buff and experienced the turbulent love that is the theme of *Werther*. In September he left Wetzlar suddenly and returned to Frankfurt.

These were exciting and fertile years for the young poet. He met many important figures in the intellectual life of Germany. His mental and emotional development was dynamic and swift. A severe illness was followed by a religious, mystical spell which drew him to pietism, alchemy, Swedenborgianism. He was involved in five serious love affairs, each of which ended unhappily.

Goethe's writings at this time comprise several volumes of lyric poetry, a dozen plays and operettas, the tragedy *Götz von Berlichingen* (his first major work), and the novel *The Sufferings of Young Werther*. Many other works were begun, including the prototypes for *Faust* and *Wilhelm Meister*.

In 1775 Goethe received and accepted an invitation from Duke Carl August of Weimar to visit Weimar. Goethe went there as a companion to the young duke. He settled in Weimar and became involved in the political life of the duchy. He served as a high official of the administration, with a seat in the Privy Council, as minister of war and finances. For ten years he was prime minister of the state. He directed the Court theater and produced many of the plays performed in it.

In this period he began serious studies in science—geology and mineralogy, meteorology, botany and anatomy—and in 1784 discovered the existence of the intermaxillary bone in man. Emotionally, the important experience of the decade was his relationship to Charlotte von Stein, a woman of deep culture, who influenced him profoundly for the good. He wrote steadily: poems, the first (prose) version of *Iphigenia in Tauris*, the first version of *Wilhelm Meister* (*Wilhelm Meister's Theatrical Mission*), the first version of *Torquato Tasso*. And again he traveled extensively.

In 1786 Goethe left Weimar quietly for Italy, where he spent the next two years, principally in Rome. Here he completed his tragedy *Egmont*, rewrote *Iphigenia in Tauris* in verse, finished *Tasso*, and added a number of scenes to his *Faust*.

After returning to Weimar, he withdrew from affairs of state and devoted himself almost wholly to letters and science and the theater. He lived with Christiane Vulpius, who bore him a son; he did not marry her until 1806. In 1790 he went to Italy for the second time. Two years later he accompanied the Duke's forces to France in the war against the Revolutionary army. He was present at the cannonade of Valmy and at the siege of Mainz and recorded his impressions in his *Campaign in France*.

In 1794 began the friendship with Schiller, which lasted until the latter's death in 1805. The two poets spurred each other to literary activity and collaborated on a series of satirical epigrams (*Xenien*). The literary fruits of this period include the second version of *Wilhelm Meister* (*Wilhelm Meister's Apprentice Years*), the epic poem *Hermann and Dorthea* (a love story set against the background of the French Revolution), translations of Benvenuto Cellini's autobiography and of works by Voltaire and Diderot. Several major works begun at this time (the epic *Achilleis* and the drama *The Natural Daughter*) remained fragments. What is now the first part of *Faust* appeared in 1808. Goethe's scientific studies yielded two treatises on the science of optics and a section of his treatise on the theory of colors (*Zur Farbenlehre*).

The remainder of Goethe's life was uneventful and progressively saddened by a series of deaths. Schiller died in 1805, Goethe's mother in 1808, his wife Christiane in 1816, Frau von Stein in 1827, the Duke in 1828, Goethe's only son August in 1830. In 1814 he fell in love with Marianne von Willemer, a young woman of considerable literary talent, some of whose poems Goethe incorporated into his *West-Eastern Divan*. In 1823, at the age of seventy-four, he suffered an intense passion for Ulrike von Levetzow and wished to marry the young girl.

The principal writings of the last years are *The Elective Affinities* (1809); a volume of poems in the oriental manner of the Persian poet Hafis, entitled *The West-Eastern Divan* (1814–1819); *Wilhelm Meister's Travels* (1821); several autobiographical works *Fiction and Truth* (1809–1831), and *Italian Journey* (1817). There was much poetry besides that of the *Divan*, mostly reflective in character. Even before the publication of the first part of *Faust* in 1808, Goethe had been writing portions of what was to become the second part of the poem. The *Helena* (Act III) dates from 1800; the poem was finished in 1831, a few months before the poet's death.

Goethe became a legendary figure even during his lifetime. There was a steady flow of visitors to Weimar, including non-Germans like Mme de Staël, Emerson, Thackeray. The young poet Heine visited him in 1824 and recorded his impression of the great man only half ironically:

That correspondence between personality and genius which we expect to find in extraordinary men was wholly present in Goethe. His physical appearance was just as significant as the word that animated his writings; his figure, too, was harmonious, clear, joyful, nobly proportioned, and one could study Greek art from it as from an ancient statue. Goethe's eyes remained just as divine in his old age as they had been in his youth. Though time was able to cover his head with snow, it could not bow it. He bore it as always, upright and proud, and when he spoke, he grew in height, and when he stretched out his hand, it seemed as if he could prescribe with his finger the course which the stars should follow in the sky. People claimed that they noticed a cold trait of egoism about his mouth; but this trait, too, is characteristic of the eternal gods, indeed of the father of the gods, the great Jupiter, with whom I have already compared Goethe. Really, when I visited him in Weimar and stood facing him, I involuntarily looked to the side to see whether the eagle was not there, too, with the lightning in his beak. I was on the point of addressing him in Greek, but since I noticed that he understood German, I told him that the plums on the road from Jena to Weimar tasted good. In the many long winter nights I had pondered deeply on the many sublime and profound things I would tell the great Goethe if I ever got to see him. And when I finally saw him I told him that the Saxon plums tasted very good. And Goethe smiled. He smiled with those same lips which had once kissed the fair Leda, Europa, Danae, Semele, and so many other princesses or just plain nymphs.

Goethe carried on a voluminous correspondence and kept diaries. His scientific studies have earned him a modest place in the history of biology and the geologists have named a mineral after him (Goethite). He was an ardent collector of art objects and a painter. During his first Italian journey alone he produced more than a thousand landscapes. He founded and directed several journals. The standard edition of his works, the *Weimarausgabe,* comprises 140 volumes. There are several chronicles of his life in calendar form; they take about a hundred pages each to record the events of his life and the titles of his works.

Afterword

In May 1772 Goethe arrived in Wetzlar, an old Imperial town on the river Lahn, the seat of the Supreme Court of the Holy Roman Empire. Young lawyers went there to acquire their final polish, and the more important members of the Reich maintained embassies. Following the wishes of his overbearing father, the young graduate from law school inscribed himself as a probationer at the Imperial Court.

But Goethe had no more genuine interest in the law now than he had displayed during his student days. It was literature that drew him and the society of people who would be raw material for the man of letters. He attached himself to a group of young lawyers and diplomats who met at a local inn for talk and jest. Goethe was the youngest among them, but he stood out at once as a brilliant eccentric who, moreover, commanded respect as the author of some published verse and of a still unpublished drama about the medieval knight, Götz von Berlichingen.

Several weeks later, on June 9th, Goethe met Charlotte Buff at a dance in the nearby village of Volpertshausen, virtually under the same circumstances as those in which Werther meets Charlotte (letter of June 16, 1771). He was deeply in love almost at once—before he knew that the girl was already betrothed to Johann Christian Kestner, secretary in one of the embassies at Wetzlar. For the young man of twenty-two it was his fourth love, if that word may be used to cover the various degrees of emotional commitment which he had experienced up to this time. His passion developed approximately like Werther's in the first book of the novel. Some of the scenes described there actually occurred. The tension between Werther and Albert is a piece of life, though Kestner was a far more admirable person than the Albert whom Goethe put into the novel. Early in September Goethe realized that Charlotte was wholly devoted to Kestner and would never give him anything but friendship. After a final meeting with the two lovers (a meeting that is fairly literally transcribed in the last letter of Book One, September 10, 1771) Goethe packed his bags and left

Wetzlar without saying good-by, leaving behind a note for Kestner and one for Charlotte, in which he described his desperate state of mind.

He went up the Rhine to Ehrenbreitstein, where he was introduced into the La Roche family. He found consolation in the company of Sophie La Roche, the novelist, and even more in that of her sixteen-year-old daughter Maximiliane, with the wonderful black eyes that made him forget Charlotte temporarily. Back in Frankfurt he was visited by Kestner, and the old wound began to bleed again. He bombarded the couple with letters which frankly avowed his love for Charlotte. Two months later his passion drove him to Wetzlar for a few days. The visit accomplished nothing; he left in an emotional state that was in no way relieved or improved.

Late in November he heard from Kestner about the suicide of Carl Wilhelm Jerusalem, which had occurred on October 30th. Goethe had known Jerusalem casually when they were both students at Leipzig; he had seen Jerusalem at Wetzlar occasionally; he felt deeply enough about the gifted young man's tragic end to ask Kestner for a full account of it. Many details from Kestner's report went into Goethe's description of Werther's death. Jerusalem, who was the secretary of the Braunschweig legation at Wetzlar, had been a melancholiac by temperament. He had been badly treated by a superior officer in the service; and he was involved in a hopeless passion for the wife of a colleague. These factors together had made life intolerable for him. In a letter to Sophie La Roche, dated November 1772, Goethe describes Jerusalem's end, basing himself on a report he received from Baron Kielmannsegg, in terms that apply to Werther. "The most anguished striving for truth and moral goodness undermined his heart to such a degree that failures in life and passion drove him to take mournful resolution." It was the tragic story of Jerusalem's suicide which supplied Goethe with a "fable" for his own unhappy experience in Wetzlar.

In April of 1773 Kestner married Charlotte in Wetzlar. Goethe knew of the event in advance, was in constant touch with the couple, insisted on ordering the wedding rings for them, and revealed in his letters a state of profound agitation, which was only increased by the marriage. But in January 1774 Maximiliane Brentano, née La Roche, she of the black eyes, came to live in Frankfurt as the wife of a wholesale grocer, a man more than twice her age and who shared none of her intellectual or aesthetic interests. The young wife of eighteen became the stepmother of five children and lived in an apartment above her husband's business. Goethe began to frequent the house; ardent scenes ensued between Tristan and Isolde, which King Mark did not relish. A month later the young lawyer and writer was forbidden to enter the Brentano house.

The materials for the novel *Die Leiden des jungen Werther* were there; they assembled themselves rapidly in Goethe's mind and took shape as one of the classics of world literature. Without making a plan, merely rereading the letters he had written to his friend Merck and Kestner's report to him about the suicide of Jerusalem, Goethe began to write. In a few weeks the book was finished; it was sent to a publisher at Leipzig, and appeared at Michaelmas of 1774.

What drew Goethe to Charlotte is described in *Werther*: the fact that her sedate, steady character was the antipode of his turbulent one; she seemed to offer him that peace of mind he so sorely needed. This turbulence Goethe himself acknowledged many years later in his autobiography, *Dichtung und Wahrheit* (*Fiction and Truth*). What he says there is corroborated by his friends and acquaintances of the "Werther" years. Goethe's emotional turmoil during this period is attested to in his letters and in the tone and mood and even the content of his early writings. His mental condition during this time, as we gather from his own repeated statements—both direct and oblique—in his writings, was characterized by terrible loneliness, by the inability to focus his mind on what he was doing, and by a rapid alternation between the extremes of joy and grief, pleasure and pain, idealism and despair. His ambivalence admits into the same breast superiority, conceit, arrogance—to the point of contempt for the opinion of others—and submissiveness and diffidence close to despair. He is self-centered and domineering and, therefore, unpopular; but he is also pliable and sensitive to the climate that surrounds him and careful not to ruffle sensibilities. Consequently, even those who shake their heads about him are consumed with reverence and adoration and predict greatness for him in extravagant terms. "Emotion running riot," "a chaos of feeling"—these are the terms which students of Goethe apply to his pre-Weimar personality. He is unstable in temperament, in the life he leads, in the work he produces. Barker Fairley finds him intellectually immature in comparison with other poets like Keats, Shelley, or Hölderlin. And Emil Staiger, commenting on the fragmentary nature of his early writings, on the fact that he began so much and finished almost nothing, asks: "Has any other writer made such a spendthrift, planless beginning?" Goethe compares himself to Cain, Tantalus, Philoctetes, Orestes, St. Sebastian. He repeatedly reverts to the images of the chameleon, the weathercock, the peep show (*Raritätenkasten*), to a ship in a storm, to describe himself and the literary characters who are the projections of his own image in the writings of these years. And the thought of suicide is often in his mind as the only release from the unhappiness that consumes him.

This state lasted about ten years (1765–1775) and was accompanied by a serious physical breakdown, the nature of which has never been precisely determined. The best description of Goethe's mental state is that given by Barker Fairley in *A Study of Goethe* (pp. 4–59); this able critic and admirer of Goethe does not shrink from employing the term "pathological" to characterize Goethe's state of mind. The harsh word is justified; but it should not be forgotten that this same disturbed, pathological young man had obtained a solid education, had taken a law degree, was actually practicing law (in however desultory a fashion), was creating literature of high excellence—including lyric poetry that has remained within the canon of the world's best. And the evidence is there in abundance that, even before he became the famous author of *Werther*, Goethe impressed his contemporaries, to the point of extravagant enthusiasm, by his striking personality and abilities.

Goethe was not alone in this turbulence of mind. These "Werther" years (c. 1765–1785) are known in the history of German literature as the period of *Sturm und Drang* (Storm and Stress). It was an era of violent emotional reaction against the intellectualism of the Enlightenment (*Aufklärung*). The course of this rebellion parallels similar movements in England and France; indeed, it received a strong impetus from those parallel developments. A wave of emotionalism had already inundated the *Aufklärung* itself; in Germany it began about 1740 and rose steadily through the following decades, as *Aufklärung* merged into *Sturm und Drang*. The English weeklies like the *Spectator*, *Tatler*, and *Rambler*; the novels of Richardson, Sterne, and Goldsmith; the lugubrious poetry of the "graveyard school"; the "tearful comedy" of Destouches and Nivelle de La Chaussée, and the bourgeois tragedy of Diderot; above all, the writings of Rousseau—all these were influences which combined with native German tradition and the legacy of Pietism to promote the rebellion against cold Augustan reason, classical control, and "good taste", in the name of freedom, individualism, and emotion.

In an important essay on *Werther*, Wolfgang Kayser has called attention to the fact that the young generation of rebels had developed a new picture of reality, based on Leibniz' monadolagy and pietism, both of which bestowed final authority on the individual soul, which they saw as a microcosm that reflects the whole universe—a unique, living entity, with its own growth, course, and destiny. When Goethe saw Frau von Stein's silhouette in 1774, he exclaimed, "It would be a splendid spectacle to see how the world is mirrored in this soul." Such a soul would not reflect the splendor of universally binding truths, nor the glory of a beyond, compared to which this world is as nothing, nor a revelation given by God, but the feelings and intuitions that arise within itself out of the divine power that is latent in man.

In an early review of a volume of poems, the young Goethe castigates the superficiality of the poet's love affairs and of the girl who is the object of his love. The reviewer then erupts into a rhapsody on true love as experienced by an ideal couple with rich, warm, sensitive hearts, so rich and full that they cannot associate with one-sided people. They are creatures with "soul" (a cliché of the period)—drenched in emotion, glowing with fire in their striving and, above all, in their intuitive powers; for intuition is the meeting place between the divine within us (the soul) with the divine outside ourselves. Not only do such lovers experience the most intense rapture, but they encounter together the highest that is vouchsafed to man to experience.

Sturm und Drang is the first stage in the evolution of German romanticism, and it already shows all the later basic attitudes that we associate with romantic sensibility: enthusiasm for the natural, the rustic, and the primitive; rebellion against rules and bonds, tradition and authority (political, social, religious); the cult of extreme individualism—indeed of extremism in general, symbolized by the yearning to break through the bounds of the finite and settle for nothing less than the infinite. Instead of the one-sided cult of intellect favored by the Enlightenment, the *Sturm und Drang* generation sought *Ganzheit*, totality of experience, an adumbration of the romantic ideal which wished to achieve a synthesis of all the faculties and all the arts. It even bore within itself the paradox that characterized later romanticism: along with rebellion against tradition went a reverence for the national past.

The artistic credo of the *Sturm und Drang* was also basically that of later romanticism. The young titans rebelled against the neo-classical canon of good taste, based on rules. Against these rules they championed originality, native genius, organic growth rather than mechanical regularity; they wanted free scope for the imagination and feelings; they showed enthusiasm for the "interesting," the "picturesque," the rustic, the irregular, the rugged, the sublime as opposed to the "beautiful" (to which the eighteenth century assigned the attributes of regularity, symmetry, balance, correct size, and polish). The *Sturm und Drang* ideal of literary diction approximated that which Wordsworth later championed: the language of every day, the homely realism of the common man, the loose syntax of natural speech. Much of the power of Goethe's *Werther* derives from its diction, which conforms to the spirit of *Sturm und Drang* aesthetics.

This elaborate excursion into the historical background of *Werther*, into Goethe's personal involvement in the events and sentiments that form the raw material of his novel, requires some justification. The "biographical heresy" has been out of favor for some time in literary criticism. The new critics would have us pay no attention to the external circumstances in a writer's life nor to the *Zeitgeist* as possible guides to an interpretation of the created work of art. "The play's the thing"; nothing else matters. Goethe himself, in the *Westöstlicher Divan*, berated the "anecdote hunters" who wish to see a *roman à clef* in every work of imaginative literature. But Goethe also made the oft-quoted statement that all his writings were fragments of a great confession. He meant that he was a subjective writer who used the raw materials which his own life had provided for him as the thematic content of his art, who created out of his personal experience rather than from a sheer empathic imagination. In his own activity as a literary critic Goethe was an early, perhaps the first, champion of the genetic method, which assumes that an awareness of the constellation that came together in the production of a work of art does help to enhance our aesthetic appreciation of the work. The preliminary sketches of a great painter, the notebooks of Beethoven which show the evolution of a phrase into a motif, the *brouillons* of Flaubert's *Madame Bovary*, are all pertinent to intelligent appreciation of the finished work. When we have studied the various elements that Goethe pulled together to make his *Werther*, our aesthetic appreciation is bound to be the more intense. Consider, for instance, the last two sentences in the novel. Goethe took them from Kestner's report on the suicide of Jerusalem. The fact that Goethe realized their climactic value and put them at the very end of the tragic history gives us an insight into his genius that would otherwise be lacking; we can appreciate Goethe's skill as an artist when we see what he did with Kestner's report. The profound value in retracing the history of *Werther* comes from following Goethe's mind as his creative imagination weaves a pattern out of these disparate elements involving external events in the lives of three separate groups of people (Goethe and the Kestners; Jerusalem and his colleague,

Goethe and the Brentanos), but even more in observing with what wonderful skill and artistry he introduced into this plot the intellectual and emotional factors that move these characters in this great tragic drama.

For *Werther* is a drama. Goethe first thought of writing it in dramatic form; and though what we now have is a subjective, "lyrical" presentation of a chain of events, seen almost entirely from the point of view of the hero-victim, there is intense drama everywhere in these pages, a constant state of conflict between protagonists, one of whom is always Werther, while the other is sometimes Albert, sometimes Wilhelm (the recipient of the letters), whose function it is to urge Werther to exercise control and common sense, or Werther's superior the Count, or the aristocratic group whom he offends, or the society with which he is constantly at odds. Even Lotte may be regarded as his antagonist, for she, like everyone else, places limits on his emotional expansion.

We have drama, too, inasmuch as the action of the novel may be divided into two acts, each with its cycle of initial calm, rising to a climax of excitement, and ending in a resolution of the conflict. Because Goethe ultimately did not choose to tell his story in the form of dialogue, he was able to exploit the relationship between Werther and the nature that surrounds him to a degree that the dramatic form would have made impossible.

But what is the theme of this drama? With some notable exceptions among the more discriminating, generations saw in it the sentimental tale of a young man who cannot take defeat in love, who commits suicide because he can't "get the girl." They could, like Napoleon, wallow in the romance of it and possibly emulate Werther's behavior or, like Thackeray, ridicule the silly lover:

> Werther had a love for Charlotte,
> Such as words could never utter,
> Would you know how first he met her?
> She was cutting bread and butter.
>
> Charlotte was a married lady,
> And a moral man was Werther,
> And for all the wealth of Indies
> Would do nothing that might hurt her.
>
> So he sighed and pined and ogled,
> And his passion boiled and bubbled;
> Till he blew his silly brains out,
> And no more was by them troubled.
>
> Charlotte, having seen his body
> Borne before her on a shutter,
> Like a well-conducted person
> Went on cutting bread and butter.

Today we know better. *Werther* is not primarily a novel about a tragic love, but a profound character study of a psychological type who has become more and more central in our Western culture: the alienated or frustrated man, who cannot find a place for himself in society; for whom all life turns sour and the world becomes a prison; in whom these sentiments or attitudes assume pathological intensity. Goethe himself supplied the key to his intentions in a terse note written almost immediately after he had finished the original version of the novel. On June 1, 1774, he described it as "a novel in which I depict a young person who, endowed with profound and pure sensibility and true penetration, loses himself in romantic dreams, undermines himself through speculation, until finally, deranged by added unhappy passions— specifically an infinite love— puts a bullet through his head." It is clear that Goethe saw in the love motif in *Werther* no more than an illustration of Werther's general character.

The skill with which Goethe makes Werther reveal himself in the early letters is one of the strong features of the novel. In a most natural way Werther exposes the principal traits of his character to us before he ever sees Lotte. If we go back to these early letters, we can see with what inevitability his later fate develops.

The fundamental trait in Werther's character is his emotionalism. He is a man of feeling, with a noble scorn for the rationalism of his age as it is embodied in Albert. ". . . my heart," Werther writes in the letter of May 9, 1772, "which is really my sole pride, and which alone is the source of everything, of all my strength, all my bliss, and all my misery. Ah, what I know, everyone can know—my heart is mine alone." And in the argument with Albert on the subject of suicide (August 12, 1771), he throws down the gauntlet to the smug, sensible rationalists. "Oh you sensible people!" he exclaims with a smile. "Passion! Drunkenness! Madness! You stand there so calm, so unsympathetic, you moral people. You condemn the drunkard, abhor the man bereft of his reason, pass by like the priest and thank God like the pharisee that He did not make you as one of these." When Albert condemns suicide on the conventional grounds that it is a cowardly way of evading the responsibilities of life, Werther counters heatedly that it is, on the contrary, an act of exemplary courage like that of a rebel against an unbearable tyranny. And he makes a generalization that is of singular importance for understanding his psyche: "If effort is strength, why should supreme effort be the opposite?" In other words, he despises moderation as a sign of weakness; for passion is to him not a vice, but a higher degree of emotion and, therefore, a good thing. In his thinking he anticipates Nietzsche and modern psychology which recognizes that much bourgeois moderation has its source in timidity and cowardice (*Thus Spake Zarathustra*: "Of the Pale Criminal"). Friedrich Gundolf, in fact, described Werther as a "titan of feeling," a companion to other Goethean figures of this period, to Prometheus the titan of creativity, to Caesar the titan of activity, to Faust the titan of effort.

What values does Werther's heart dictate to him? Foremost, perhaps, a powerful feeling for nature in all her moods. The second letter in the book contains the magnificent apotheosis to verdant nature, one of many such glorious tributes in the work. But Werther savors nature in her stormy and gloomy moods as well. Nature gives him that same feeling of expansion, of harmony with the cosmic order, that Wordsworth recorded so memorably. She also offers him relief from the tension which is his normal state. The progress of his malady is reflected in the novel in the changed face of nature. In Book Two Werther sees her no longer in her happy moods but in her gloomy and threatening aspects. If this side of nature gives him comfort too, it is a masochistic comfort, the wry pleasure that the hypochondriac derives from the fact that all is unwell.

Werther is a man of nature in another sense too—in the Rousscauistic sense of championing the natural against the artificial conventions of society. He loves children and the common people, the downtrodden, the "innocent" criminal; he loves simplicity, naïveté, the primitive, the original, persecuted genius.

The insult to his dignity which Werther suffers at the hands of the aristocratic circle in which he moves—one of the central motifs of the novel—brings out this Rousseauistic quality in his character. That these empty-headed aristocrats should reject him as an unfit associate merely because he was not born with a handle to his name is an affront to nature. That his pedantic superior in office should censure his vivid, dynamic style in favor of mechanically correct syntax and vocabulary is equally unendurable to him. For in art, too, Werther is a man of feeling. Art should express emotion, not be shaped by reason. Accordingly, in his very first letter he praises the late Count's garden because it bears the marks of having been laid out by a feeling heart rather than a cold, scientific mind. He brushes off with lofty contempt the neoclassical respect for rules in art. A man who follows the rules will produce a "correct" work of art, just as a good bourgeois who obeys the rules of society will live a correct life. But how barren this is in comparison with the dynamic, though unbridled, life of the genius, or the vigorous, expressive, natural (though irregular) work of art of the Promethean creator.

But all this does not necessarily lead to a prognosis of suicide. After all, the history of human endeavor is filled with rebels against mass values who lived out their lives and repaid humanity for its neglect and hostility by bequeathing to posterity great works of art or thought or statesmanship.

What makes the difference in Werther's case is two further features of his character: his urge to infinity and his inner disharmony.

Werther's statement, quoted above, about effort and supreme effort, is an expression of his extremism. For the common-sense answer to his logic is that experience shows us repeatedly that an excess of even a good thing may be bad. But Werther is what is now called a perfectionist; nothing but the extreme, the absolute, will satisfy him. And since the search for the absolute is bound to end in frustration, he is perpetually frustrated in life. Even his adored nature becomes a disappointment to him; she cannot offer him lasting satisfaction. For in her, too, he sees a revelation of that infinity which is his ideal; but later on he finds that the glorious nature he so adored is nothing but a lacquered picture, without life; and he can no longer live in her, but stands aside and observes her apathetically.

For Werther the outside world is but a reflection of his inner mental state. Things exist only in the meaning which he assigns to them. He is one of the first of those modern men whose attitude is summed up in the words of Schopenhauer: the world is my representation. Since this inner representation is on a high level, reality fails him at every point. "Our power of imagination, compelled by its nature to sublimate itself, nourished by the fantastic images of literature, creates a series of beings of whom we are the lowest, and everything outside ourselves seems more splendid to us, everyone else more perfect than we are. The process is a perfectly natural one" (October 20, 1771). His lot is perpetual disillusionment: in nature, in his association with his fellow men, in love. This subjectivity in his approach to life is expressed in one of his favorite images: life is a dream; in his predilection for the half-light, his will to illusion. A consequence of this subjectivism is that he never seriously blames himself for his failures and his unhappiness; it is always the fault of society or of the world order, of that *Schicksal* (destiny), which plays an altogether disproportionate role in German thinking.

This subjectivism leads to a slighting of reality. For one thing,

Werther can only see the restrictions which are put in the way of his will to achieve. Besides, the rhythm of life as it is lived by ordinary people becomes trivial to him; time and energy are wasted in carrying out the pointless chores of daily existence. We are on the way to the absurd universe of the existentialists.

As the universe becomes trivial, so Werther himself grows more and more exalted. Commentators on the novel have noted the Biblical language which Werther applies to himself in his later letters. He draws parallels, in situation and language, between his fate and that of Jesus as recorded in the Gospel of John. An examination of the relevant passages makes it clear that Werther regards himself as suffering a martyrdom similar to that of Jesus; he, too, is an innocent victim of human malevolence; he, too, is abandoned by God and goes to join God the Father in Heaven. This analogy is all the more striking as Werther is not an orthodox Christian, not a churchgoer, even rejecting altogether the mediation of Christ. To a Christian reader this identification of himself with Christ must seem blasphemy, unless it be interpreted as the excrescence of a disordered mind. If we remember that Werther was conceived as a warning rather than an example, it is clear that this latter interpretation is the one which Goethe intended to be taken from this Biblical analogy. He wished to show the logical end to which Wertherism leads. What more striking way could he have chosen to do so?

When we speak of a titan, we think of an indomitable, intrepid fighter like Prometheus or Oedipus. A titan seeks to break through the limitations which nature, his environment, his fellowmen—indeed the gods themselves—have placed in his path. Does Werther qualify for this distinction? Hardly. His passivity has often been noted. He himself more than once speaks of his emotional waywardness as a failing. Near the very beginning of the novel (May 13, 1771) he writes to Wilhelm: "You have never seen anything so uneven, so unsteady as this heart." And he continues in the same vein, referring to his oscillations between the poles of euphoria and melancholy, concluding that he pampers his heart as one pampers an ailing child, granting its every wish.

Goethe took great pains to underscore the weaknesses in Werther's character; he emerges as anything but a titanic being. His lofty superiority to all the philistines he encounters and his sense of self-righteousness in every situation are but the surface camouflage for a deep feeling of insecurity which he recognizes as existing at the core of his being. "When we feel inadequate to ourselves, every-

thing seems inadequate to us" (August 22, 1771). "Good Lord,
Who have given me all this, why did You not withhold half of it
and give me self-confidence and contentment? . . . We feel so often
that we lack many things, and the very things we lack someone else
often seems to us to possess, and we also attribute to him all that
we have ourselves, and a certain ideal contentment into the bargain" (October 20, 1771).

In a brilliant study entitled *The Blind Man and the Poet*, E. M.
Wilkinson and L. A. Willoughby have pointed out that Goethe's
novel conveys its "message" structurally as well as by argument.
They call attention to the fact that Lessing's tragedy *Emilia Galotti* is mentioned at two crucial spots in *Werther*: at the very
beginning and at the end of the novel. In his second letter
Werther laments his inability to draw even a line, although "I have
never been a greater painter than I am in these moments." He
claims to possess the artist's inner vision, and this alone matters,
not the execution. Now this passage is a paraphrase of a similar
statement made by the painter Conti in Act I, Scene 4 of Lessing's
play. The authors make it clear that Conti's views do not represent
Lessing's. On the contrary; Lessing, like his contemporary Herder,
refused to accept such a dichotomy between vision and execution,
agreeing with the ancient Greek assumption that feeling, purpose,
and skill must be one. Anyone who arrogates to himself the title of
artist or master without being able to demonstrate his mastery
through concrete achievement, is a *Schwärmer*, a dreamer or
"enthusiast," in the eighteenth-century sense of that word: someone who is out of touch with reality to his own peril. What is true
for the artist is no less valid for man in general; enthusiasm, the
"tendency to exalt that which is within—whether desire, ideal,
motive, theory, system or abstraction—at the expense of that which
is without, to press impatiently for immediate realization of what
the mind can envisage while ignoring the claims of the factual situation"—such extremism (which Bernard Shaw attacked in Ibsen's
name as "idealism") can only lead to catastrophe. Wilkinson and
Willoughby argue that the very plot and structure of Lessing's tragedy demonstrate the tragic consequences of *Schwärmerei*. This
lesson the young Goethe had already learned in 1771 during his
meeting with Herder in Strassburg. *Emilia Galotti* appeared in
1772; in it he found the same basic idea expressed obliquely, structurally, in a work of art. This explains the inclusion of a minor
detail in the final paragraphs of *Werther*: "*Emilia Galotti* lay open
on his desk." Werther, Goethe wishes to tell us, had read the play

but missed its point; Goethe himself did understand its import. By his two allusions to Lessing's tragedy, placed so strategically, he underscored the meaning of his novel: that it is a study of tragic *Schwärmerei*.

It is difficult, in writing about Goethe's *Werther*, to avoid using the psychological jargon of our day; for some basic syndromes which modern psychiatry has made familiar to us are strikingly anticipated in the book. Two thorough studies—one by Ernst Feise in 1926, the other by Stuart Atkins in 1948, both elaborately documented—have explored the manifestations of depth psychology in Goethe's novel. From them Werther emerges as a neurotic character, suffering from a strong sense of inferiority, which he attempts to overcome by making a masculine protest through nonconformity, rebellion, and contempt for his fellow men—to whom he applies such unflattering epithets as "dogmatic puppets," "fools," "rogues," "dogs," "weird eccentrics," "funny faces." The whole letter of May 22, 1771, is a studied insult to average humanity. And this is the Werther who boasts of his love for the common folk. He is a highly self-centered narcissist, who refers all events and all values back to his own interest. He parades as a political and social revolutionary, and as such he is regarded by his contemporaries; but how much genuine principle is there behind his profession? For instance, he is not against class distinction as such, but only against those distinctions which work against him. His naturalistic or "biological" view of human relations meets his subjective needs. For him all nature shows a perpetual interacting between opposing forces, both material and spiritual, some creative, others destructive. This necessary interaction of forces is what we call destiny; both our physical and mental life are the products of natural laws over which the human will has little control. It is, therefore, meaningless, in his view, to apply ethical judgments to human behavior; one can at best trace it back to its causes and seek to "understand" it. This is a philosophy of life that is tailored to the needs of a weak-willed man, which Werther is. Stuart Atkins draws up a catalogue of Werther's accomplishments during the eighteen months covered by the action of the novel; it is not impressive. Ernst Feise goes further still and suggests that Werther has the will to fail. He cunningly sets himself goals that are impossible for him to attain, so that he need not exert himself to attain them. He can always console himself with the thought that he had the best intentions, and blame society or the environment for frustrating them. He can then indulge himself in the negative satisfaction of the hypochondriac who enjoys his bad health and his failures.

This is also the pattern of his behavior in his affair with Lotte. If Werther is really so superior to Albert as he thinks he is, and if Lotte is the discriminating person he thinks she is, why does he not make a positive gesture to take her away from Albert before the marriage? We know from Kestner's diary that the real Charlotte had made it quite clear to the young Goethe that her lot was definitely tied to that of Kestner and that her interest in Goethe did not go beyond that of friendship. The Lotte of the novel is by no means so single-minded, either before or after her marriage, and even less so in the first version of the book. Why, then, doesn't Werther exploit his conviction that Lotte is not indifferent to him? His correspondent Wilhelm puts this question to him and he replies to it in the letter of August 8, 1771. He tells Wilhelm that he will not be speared on the horns of an "either-or" dilemma. Can one expect, he asks, that a person suffering from a lingering disease shall suddenly thrust a dagger into his bosom and put an end to his torment? Does not his very disease rob him of the power to do something to liberate himself from its ravages? And then he replies to another objection raised by Wilhelm: is it not preferable to lose one diseased limb and save the rest of the organism? He evades this. But it is significant that he has, in this discussion with Wilhelm, examined only the one of the two alternatives offered him: he has considered the "or" but not the "either." The idea that he might win Lotte away from Albert is not touched upon. Feise's suggestion that he no more wants to succeed in this venture than in any other is indeed plausible. During their last stormy interview Lotte says to him: "I fear it is only the impossibility of possessing me that makes your desire for me so strong." H. A. Korff has an apt comment to make on this situation: Werther gives the impression of savoring the pain which his unhappy love affords him, so that he may not feel the terrible inner emptiness which increasingly takes possession of him as he goes through life.

Werther's constant need of excitement, change, and novelty makes the normal man's rhythm of tension and relaxation unacceptable to him. Like Faust, he has two souls within his breast, each pulling in opposite directions. Basically, we have in Werther that ambivalence of attitude which Thomas Mann later made familiar to us through his gallery of artist-intellectuals who feel both superior and inferior to the run-of-the-mill bourgeois, or whose superiority is merely a cover for a fundamental feeling of inferiority. So perhaps this frantic need for change and excitement in Werther is a disguise for an underlying sloth, which is a mainspring of Werther's character. The letter of July 1, 1771, deals specifically and powerfully with this theme of sloth or ill-humor. Werther works himself into a passion against those who embitter life for their fellow men through their ill-humor. For these others he recommends an act of will power and a dose of self-control. He calls them spoil-sports, who are fundamentally dissatisfied with themselves and envious of others who live in inner peace. "We see happy people," he continues, "who have not been made happy by us and find this intolerable." He runs on for a while, using this revealing "we." Why is he so vehement on this subject, even bursting into tears? Is it because this impersonal "we" is really a very personal "I"? Is the final example which he gives of this type of sadism an instance in which he was more than a mere spectator, was in fact the actual cause of the unhappiness he describes? At any rate, we shall not go far wrong in regarding this tirade as one that is directed at the speaker himself.

For in the following month he will write about himself: "It is a catastrophe, Wilhelm, my active powers have atrophied into an uneasy indolence; I can't be idle and yet I can do nothing" (August 22, 1771). In his last letter to Wilhelm (December 20, 1772) he is more direct still: "It was simply my destiny to sadden those to whom I owed joy." Here we have the psychological mechanism at work: sloth, leading to guilt and self-condemnation, irritates him against the outside world, whereupon he proceeds to take vengeance by tormenting others. But "sadden" is an understatement. Like every masochist, he is a sadist too, however unconsciously. What a cunning revenge he takes on the couple who have thwarted his love, by the manner in which he takes his life. He blows out his brains with one of Albert's pistols, tells Lotte how happy he feels to have received it from her hands, and underscores the suggestion that his Christ-like passion is for her—he is shedding his blood in order that she may be happy with Albert! The effect of his cruel behavior is registered tersely in the third from the last sentence of the novel "Lotte's life was feared to be in danger."

I have used the medieval concept of sloth (accidie) to describe Werther's irrational, contradictory behavior. He lacks the vital energy, the Faustian drive, which characterizes Western man. In its extreme form this negative attitude to life is explained by modern psychiatry as deriving from what Freud called the "death wish," a form of aggression that turns inward against the self and leads to self-destruction.[1] It is a morbid form of an instinct that we all possess in embryo, but which in normal people is overruled by the much more powerful will to live. Where the death instinct is strong, it may express itself as

---

1. Hinsie and Campbell: *Psychiatric Dictionary*, under the entry: instinct, death.

cruelty (sadism) to those over whom the subject has power, or as cruelty against one-self (masochism) leading to self-destruction. Ignace Feuerlicht has shown that the text of *Werther* supports the thesis that such an aggressive, self-destructive psychological mechanism is at the bottom of Werther's behavior toward his environment and toward himself.[2] There can be no doubt that Goethe, like Sophocles and Shakespeare before him, anticipated certain of the fundamental insights that modern psychology has rediscovered.

If, in the course of this discussion, little has been said of the love motif, it is because this theme is no more than one concrete illustration of Werther's method of handling a problem—any problem. But it would be critical blindness to deny that the element of love plays a special role in the novel. Balzac, for instance, regarded *Werther* as a manual of love which provides a key to almost every situation of the human heart in love. That the work has so persistently been regarded as a romantic love tragedy, like *Romeo and Juliet*, is due to the fact that the love action does occupy most of the space in the book and is the principal event in it; but even more it is a tribute to Goethe's artistic powers. Himself endowed with a strong attraction to the Eternal Feminine, he knew superbly how to develop a love-entanglement and bring it to an inevitable conclusion.

There is, however, one aspect of Goethe's treatment of the love motif that may be described as novel: it is the fusion between love and religion, or the blurring of the distinction between heavenly and earthly love. Werther's love for Lotte is idealized passion in the courtly-love tradition, at least on the surface. He puts into it the spiritual energies which a Christian ought to reserve for his God and his religion. Werther tells us specifically that he is not a believing Christian; he conceives God as a creative force active in nature, to be apprehended through nature, which is, in the words of Faust, "God's living garment." The spiritual energy, which a man of Werther's sensibility must have in rich quantity, attaches itself to the object of his love, since he is too narcissistic to bestow it on anyone or anything else in life. His relation to his mother is one of unconcealed hostility; Wilhelm seems to exist for the sole purpose of receiving Werther's letters and executing various commissions for him. There is no one in Wahlheim with whom he is on a truly intimate footing except Lotte. So it is she who receives all the idealization that he is capable of giving, an idealization

2. Feuerlicht: "Werther's Suicide: Instinct, Reasons and Defense," *German Quarterly*, 51 (1978), 476–489.

which serves the further purpose of covering over the fundamentally sensual nature of his desire. This sensuality comes out in various places; but generally Werther tries to conceal it from himself by emphasizing the sacred, spiritual nature of his feeling.

A good deal has been written about Werther's "religion," but it is relevant to add one more comment on the subject. In 1939 Herbert Schoeffler published an essay arguing that in *Werther* Goethe had written a secular passion in imitation of the Passion of Christ, a serious parody of Christ's redemption of man through His sacrificial death on the Cross. Werther, too, dies a sacrificial death (if not for all mankind, at least for Albert and Lotte), so that the lovers may have a life of greater happiness. By following the Biblical account, Schoeffler argues, Goethe indicated that he regarded Werther's passion as being of equal importance with that of Christ: to sacrifice oneself for a profound love is, for modern man, as significant as Christ's otherworldly sacrifice for humanity. Werther is, in this interpretation, a good man animated by a noble passion which brings about his destruction because of the essential imperfection of the world order.

At the other end of the spectrum is Emil Staiger, who interprets Werther's turning to religion as a symptom of his malady: it is an attempt to submit once more to a way of thinking from which he has long become estranged and to murmur words of a reverent faith, which may be genuine enough, at a crucial time when emptiness stares him in the face. In other words, Staiger sees Werther's "religion" as one of those deathbed recantations which are attributed to certain eminent atheists and agnostics. Between these two extremes stands the thesis of E. L. Stahl, who also sees *Werther* as a religious novel. The central theme, in Stahl's view, is Werther's relation to God, rather than his conflict with society. Werther rejects society because he feels close to God, in immediate contact with Him, as Jesus did. So he needs no mediator between himself and God, as other men do. Hence, when both society and nature fail him, he clings to God and goes to join Him. His suicide is, therefore, not weakness, but strength. Schoeffler's view seems to be obviously wrong, inasmuch as it assumes that Goethe intended Werther to appear as an admirable character. The documentary evidence, both within and outside the text, refutes this assumption beyond dispute. If Schoeffler had argued that Werther regards himself as a Christ-like figure and his passion, in some form, parallel to that of Christ, he would have been on more solid ground; indeed, such a view is more acceptable than that of Staiger. In Werther's confused and overexcited mind a fusion develops between the most disparate elements: he mixes the sacred and the profane, the intellectual and the emotional. As Albert points out: making distinctions is not his strong point. Werther being what he is, it is very likely that, in his growing sickness, which includes wounded vanity, egoism, self-righteousness, and persecution mania, he would hit upon the analogy between his suffering and Christ's. Goethe was able to diagnose this clinically without presenting it sympathetically.

It is not unfair to interpret Goethe's intention in this sense; because Werther invests all his energy and all his idealism in this hopeless passion for Lotte, instead of diverting it, as Goethe did, into some other form of activity, whether social, personal, or aesthetic; when his passion fails, he has nothing left but suicide. Viewed from this perspective, the theme of love has a special symbolical value in the novel, and our former formulation must be revised, though it is still clear that the love motif is no more than an illustration of Werther's psychological problem. May not Goethe have been writing *pro domo*? By the time he composed *Werther*, he was already bothered by a pattern of behavior in love that had established itself in him: after an intense and whole-hearted involvement, he would withdraw and leave, even as Werther leaves at the end of the first book, though in a different spirit. May not Goethe unconsciously have depicted Werther's fate as an apology for his own behavior: if I had not extricated myself from these involvements, my character would have brought me to this?

We may now formulate the theme of *Werther* as the destruction of an extreme idealist by his contact with inexorable reality. This confrontation produces disillusionment or a series of frustrations, which lead him to question the value of life itself and ultimately to condemn it. For Werther's highly-developed inner life cannot find any external activity, any objective correlative, to balance it or use it up. We see, or Werther would have us see, a natural genius stifled by narrow convention, an artistic soul forced to live in a society of philistines, a pure and intense lover whose spiritual passion is frustrated by the circumstance that the object of his love betrays him. All these setbacks desiccate his mind, so that he feels completely dead inside, unable to respond to anything in life, and thus becomes a forerunner of that totally alienated man whom the modern existentialists have rediscovered. Since he has nothing to live for, he decides to drain the bitter cup which fate has handed him and thereby achieve a signal blood-sacrifice for those he leaves behind him.

There remains the question: what does suicide mean for Werther? Here, again, it is worth going back to Goethe's own experience. There is ample documentation to indicate that Goethe, in his Werther period, seriously contemplated suicide as an escape from his mental turmoil. He even kept a dagger at his bedside and made repeated attempts to plunge it into his breast. But as he could never get it in very far, he decided to live. He made no effort to romanticize this ultimate act of negation by ascribing to it other motives than the selfish one of escape from the intolerable burden of life. But he did introduce into both *Werther* and *Faust* a metaphysical justification for suicide. Both Werther and Faust see in this act the realization and the fulfillment of those aspirations which they have been unable to realize here on earth. They regard suicide as the only possible liberation from the finiteness of this world; it makes possible a swifter union with God in the beyond. Both Werther and Faust see death, not as the end of life, but as the beginning of a new life. If one should object that such a belief is inconsistent with Werther's and Faust's undogmatic, vague, quasi-agnostic pantheism, the answer is that they both do believe in a spiritual realm beyond earthly reality. The texts are not intelligible on any other assumption.

One might say that Werther and Faust reveal the same ambiguity on this score that Goethe showed throughout his life: an ambiguity which may be characterized as a *Weltanschauung*. Goethe lived in the moment; he was altogether a son of this world (*diesseitig*, the Germans say). Yet he repeatedly talks about a survival after life. He probably thought of this survival as no more than a spiritual immortality. In the poem "Grenzen der Menschheit" ("Limits of Mortality") he writes:

> Ein kleiner Ring
> Begrenzt unser Leben,
> Und viele Geschlechter
> Reihen sich dauernd
> An ihres Daseins
> Unendliche Kette.[1]

His very definition of God is most untheistic, secular, humanist:

> Im Innern ist ein Universum auch;
> Daher der Völker löblicher Gebrauch,
> Dass jeglicher das Beste, was er kennt,
> Er Gott, ja seinen Gott benennt,
> Ihm Himmel und Erden übergibt,
> Ihn fürchtet, und womöglich liebt.[2]

1. "A small ring limits our life, and many generations take their permanent place on the endless chain of their existence."

2. "In our inner world, too, there is a universe; hence, the laudable custom among peoples that each man gives the name God, indeed his God, to the best

And again in an epigram:

> Was der Mensch als Gott verehrt,
> Ist sein eigenstes Innere herausgekehrt.[3]

Yet this same Goethe saw the whole phenomenal world as a symbol of a spiritual principle; and more than once he used Christian conceptions, like that of an afterlife, to represent that principle.

At any rate it is clear that Werther appeals to God the Father to receive him when he leaves this world and is confident that God will indeed receive him. Nor is there for him any ethical problem in this act of suicide; for he views suicide, like everything else, from the "biological" point of view. He is a mentally sick man for whom the only remedy is suicide. He believes that he has as much moral right to make use of this cure as the physically sick man has to take the medicine that science offers him.

In his famous essay *On Naïve and Sentimental Literature,* Schiller condensed into one marvelous paragraph a critique of Goethe's *Werther.* It is quoted here as a summarizing statement of the points made in the foregoing essay in interpretation:

"A character who embraces an ideal with glowing emotion and flees from reality to wrestle with an insubstantial infinite; who is incessantly seeking outside himself what he is incessantly destroying within himself; for whom dreams alone are reality, while his experiences are mere barriers; who finally sees nothing but a barrier in his own existence and, as is natural, tears down this barrier too in order to penetrate to the true reality—this dangerous extremism of the sentimental character became the raw material for a creative writer in whom nature is at work more faithfully and more purely than in any other and who, among modern writers, has perhaps moved the least distance away from the sensuous truth of things. It is interesting to see with what happy instinct everything that provides nourishment for the sentimental character has been compressed into Werther: romantic, unhappy love, sensibility to nature, religious feelings, the spirit of philosophical contemplation; finally, if we are to forget nothing, the gloomy, formless, melancholy world of Ossian. If one adds to this in what an uninviting, indeed hostile light reality is placed, and how everything in the outside world combines to drive the tormented man back into his ideal world,

---

that he knows, hands over to Him heaven and earth, fears and, if possible, loves Him."

3. "What man reveres as God is his own inner being turned outward."

one can see no possible way in which such a character could escape
from such a circle."

The form in which Goethe chose to cast the novel has taken
nothing from the dramatic quality of its material. It enjoys the
same classical simplicity of plot as Flaubert's *Madame Bovary*,
together with the advantages accruing from the more open novel
form. It is idle to repeat all the *post factum* justifications that have
been given for the epistolary form in which the book has been cast.
The novel in letters had established itself as a fashion. Richardson's
two novels and Rousseau's *Nouvelle Héloise* were forerunners. This
is probably enough to account for Goethe's choice of the form; we
need look for no "higher necessity," as some German critics have,
to justify it. But there are additional literary factors for motivating
the decision. The epistolary form of narration allows the writer to
focus on the highlights of his story; he need not write unless he is
especially moved to do so. The fact that Goethe reproduces only
Werther's letters to Wilhelm, not those from Wilhelm to him,
adds to the dramatic intensity of the work. And when Werther's
state of mind has been burdened to the point of breaking, Goethe
brings in an editor, who narrates with epic calm what Werther
himself could only have put down in irrational frenzy.

The plot is as simple as the dramatic conflict which it carries.
After weathering some sort of emotional crisis, Werther arrives in a
new town, begins to feel happy in nature and in the human con-
tacts he makes. He meets Lotte and falls deeply in love with her.
Her fiancé arrives and the classic triangle is formed. Werther
leaves the town suddenly (Book One). He takes a diplomatic post,
but is unhappy in his relations with his superior. Moreover, he suffers an unearned insult from the petty aristocrats with whom he
associates. He, therefore, resigns his post and returns to the town in
which Lotte, now married, lives with Albert. His love for her grows;
since he sees no possibility of its fulfillment, he takes his own life
(Book Two).

To this simple plot Goethe has added a number of episodes
designed to act as parallels to the main action, or to reveal character, or just to create atmosphere: such are the episodes of the nut
trees; the peasant who experiences for his widowed employer a love
similar to Werther's; the insane flower picker; the rustic scenes; the
allusion to a former love; the relationship with Fräulein von B——.

Each of the two books is constructed dramatically: it begins with
a tense calm and rises to a climax, followed by an explosion. While
it is true that the book belongs to Werther, Goethe has neverthe-

less maintained a nice balance in distributing the lights and shadows on Albert and Lotte. He does not present a clear conflict between Werther at the one end of the seesaw and Albert and Lotte at the other, but rather with Werther and Albert at either end and Lotte at the center, bending alternately in either direction (though quite unconsciously), so that our suspense is maintained throughout the action. For, with all her resolution and straightforwardness and sound, bourgeois morality, Lotte is a woman; she appreciates fun and male attention. Here, much more than in Lessing's Emilia Galotti, one could speculate on the "guilt" of the heroine in helping to produce the catastrophe.

It would require too much space to analyze in detail the artistic devices that Goethe uses to enhance the reader's aesthetic delight as he follows the unfolding of the action. These devices include the masterful handling of the natural landscape to create the proper atmosphere in each of Werther's varying moods; the hundreds of small allusions to men, events, and attitudes of the day—things that were familiar to the educated reader of Goethe's time, but must unfortunately be explained in footnotes today; the motivation and preparation of the principal events in the story; the gradual deterioration of Werther's own mind; the careful introduction and development of the suicide motif.

When we ask what it is in this novel that has held the attention and won the admiration of generations of sophisticated readers to this day, we are compelled to single out the rich variation in tone, imagery, and mood which the work presents. The idyllic and the rapturous, the humorous and the satirical, the casual sketching-in of genre scenes, matter-of-fact reporting, the deeply emotional descriptions of mental crisis, the worlds of Homer and Ossian and the everyday tone of modern realism—all are there in the right places and proportions.

Detailed studies have been made of the imagery and leitmotifs in which the novel abounds. There is a cluster of imagery that belongs to the preromantic world of Ossian and the folk ballad: the picturesque, the patriarchal, the idyllic; solitude, highly charged passion, the sentimental. There is the imagery taken from political struggle: freedom, prisons, chains, restriction, walls, the curtain lifted. There is the rich imagery of the Bible: God and Devil, heaven and hell, angels, prophets, saints, the blessed and the damned, pilgrims, and pharisees. But above all there is the imagery of disease and health: fever, intoxication, dizziness, madness, oppression, torment, anguish, pain, healing, comfort, balsam, and refreshment. These manifold images work like musical leitmotifs to keep the spirit of the book before the reader's mind. The title itself is a masterful example of artistic ambiguity. *Leiden* means suffering, whether physical or mental. Goethe wants to imply both; for mental suffering is for Werther a physical disease, in line with his holistic view of life. There is another type of leitmotif which pervades the work: what is called in German *"Dingsymbol,"* i.e., the symbolic use of an object. There is a recurrent reference to fountains, to Lotte's melody, to trees. Homer and Ossian are such symbols; so are the many genre pictures that dot the *Werther* landscape.

On every page there is evidence of a striving for realism: in the use of homely language, in the broken sentences to suggest high emotion, in the repetitions and stammerings, in the fiction of an editor, in the footnotes and asterisks to conceal names. *Werther* is one of the first works in European literature to be composed in spoken, as opposed to literary, language. The vocabulary and rhythm are those of the spoken language, not those of rhetoric or high literature. This feature lends the work an exemplary freshness.

Of course, only those who read *Werther* in German, especially in the first version, can savor the full effect produced by Goethe's handling of language. Herder, from whom the young Goethe learned so much, was a pioneer and seminal thinker in the whole area of linguistics. It was he who first formulated a conception of poetic diction that has retained validity to this day. As Professors Wilkinson and Willoughby point out, for Herder the special feature of the language of poetry (that is, of creative literature) consists in this: that language and thought are inseparable—"the thought clings to the expression" as Herder himself puts it—whereas in discursive writing, thought attempts, in the interest of achieving greater clarity, to liberate itself from dependence on expression. The creative writer wants to express through language not only information, thought, and emotion, but the gestures, tones, facial expressions that accompany the utterance. To do this, the language he uses must cease being merely referential and assume a "body" of its own; it must develop into a self-contained system of meaningful relations and suggestive symbols. By drawing out all the resources which language harbors within itself—sound, rhythm, sequence, even shape, as well as unusual syntax and punctuation—the poet can create, through language alone, a poetic illusion that is a symbolic expression of feeling.

Such a "symbolistic" use of language is found throughout *Werther* side by side with the realistic diction described in the previous paragraph. The two antithetical styles blend perfectly to create an atmosphere that the translator cannot reproduce in his own tongue.

But the greatest artistic triumph which Goethe achieved is to make us feel, as Thomas Mann observed, the mortal weakness of his hero as exuberant strength. Even his exit from life seems to be that of a victorious conqueror. Wolfgang Kayser argues vigorously in defense of the thesis that Werther is an admirable man. He sees nowhere a condemnation of Werther's behavior; on the contrary, Werther is depicted as a noble soul. "The youth with the highly sensitive soul is nowhere put in the wrong because of his character or his activity. His sensibility and uncompromising nature appear at all times as the noblest human endowments." Even the name that Goethe gave his hero (Werther means "worthy") is a stamp of approval. I cannot agree with this view of Kayser's; but it may well be that Goethe, realizing how much of Werther there was in himself, set out to create a hero and to vindicate him by blaming society for his fate. But his artistic eye saw clearly that the fault lay in Werther, not in his stars. As a man he felt sympathy for Werther's plight; as an artist he felt compelled to condemn him. It is only when we read the text closely that we see the pathetic creature that Goethe has put before us. To have created a character on these two levels is a triumph.

Werther became famous at once, not only in Germany but abroad too. Sentimental young men sported Werther's costume: blue coat and yellow trousers and vest; some lovelorn creatures followed his example and committed suicide with copies of the novel in their pockets.

The physician Zimmermann had to let two weeks elapse after reading the first book of the novel before he dared tackle the second. Another contemporary wrote that for four weeks he was bathed in tears, which he shed not for Werther's fate but in the contrition of his heart, in the humiliating consciousness that he could not be like this man. There has been much sneering at *Werther* as a typical product of German sentimentality. It is well to remember that the Werther craze was European in scope, that it lasted a long time—though in attenuated form—and that there was strong opposition to "Wertherism" in Germany too. There were many imitations of the novel in European literature, adaptations, parodies, attacks both from the camps of the rationalists and from narrow orthodox Christians, who saw in the work an apology of *Weltschmerz* rather than a warning against it. Kestner protested at the uncalled-for publicity which it brought him and Charlotte (those were different times!) and Goethe had some explaining to do. At first he was proud of the work; later he developed a strong aversion to it. In 1780 he reread it for the first time since its appearance and expressed astonishment at the book. Two years later he began to revise it; the revision was not completed till 1786;

it is the version which has become standard and is reprinted here. He did not read the novel again until 1824, when the publisher of the original work, Weygand of Leipzig, suggested issuing a de luxe reprint to commemorate the fiftieth anniversary of its publication and asked Goethe to write a preface to the book. Goethe read proofs of this reprint and was strengthened in the aversion which he had expressed in conversation to different people over the years. Instead of a preface he composed the poignant poem "An Werther," in which he envies his hero for having escaped from this world so early, leaving his creator to relive Werther's suffering over and over again:

> Noch einmal wagst du, vielbeweinter Schatten,
> Hervor dich an das Tageslicht,
> Begegnest mir auf neu beblümten Matten,
> Und meinen Anblick scheust du nicht.
> Es ist, als ob du lebtest in der Frühe,
> Wo uns der Tau auf Einem Feld erquickt
> Und nach des Tages unwillkommner Mühe
> Der Scheidesonne letzter Strahl entzückt;
> Zum Bleiben ich, zum Scheiden du erkoren,
> Gingst du voran—und hast nicht viel verloren.

* * *

> Du lächelst, Freund, gefühlvoll, wie sich ziemt:
> Ein grässlich Scheiden machte dich berühmt;
> Wir feierten dein kläglich Missgeschick,
> Du liessest uns zu Wohl and Weh zurück.
> Dann zog uns wieder ungewisse Bahn
> Der Leidenschaften labyrinthisch an;
> Und wir, verschlungen wiederholter Not,
> Dem Scheiden endlich—Scheiden ist der Tod!
> Wie klingt es rührend, wenn der Dichter singt,
> Den Tod zu meiden, den das Scheiden bringt!
> Verstrickt in solche Qualen, halbverschuldet,
> Geb ihm ein Gott zu sagen, was er duldet.[4]

For Goethe was once more involved in a hopeless love—this time for the young Ulrike von Levetzow.

---

4. "Once more you venture, much bewept shadow, forth into the light of day, confront me on new flowering meadows, and do not retreat before my view. It is as if you were living in the early morning, when the dew refreshes us on one field, and after the unwelcome effort of the day the last ray of the parting sun delights us; I—chosen to stay, you to depart; you went ahead—and did not lose much. . . .

"You smile, friend, with deep feeling, as is proper: a gruesome parting made you famous; we celebrated your wretched misfortune, you left us behind for weal and woe. Then the uncertain, labyrinthine path of the passions drew us once more; and we, entwined in repeated distress, finally for parting—parting is death! How touching it sounds when the poet sings, to avoid the death which parting brings! Enmeshed in such torments, half involved in guilt, may a god give him the power to say what he endures."

In seeking to account for the unending popularity that *Werther* has enjoyed we must realize that Goethe made a good choice of material. The Werther malady was particularly rife throughout the romantic period of European literature. This is shown not only by the high regard in which Goethe's work was held, but by the many imitations that appeared during the following half-century. It is, therefore, rather futile for German historians of literature to seek an explanation for its hold on people in the conditions of German life and thought that existed in the Werther years; this could at best account for the book's popularity in its own day. Goethe himself saw more deeply when he told Eckermann in 1824 that *Werther* captures a definite situation in the life of young people everywhere and at all times. Wertherism, in other words, is a world phenomenon, not a provincial, eighteenth-century German affair.

But the most fundamental question is: why is it Goethe's *Werther* that has survived and not the romantic heroes of Benjamin Constant or Ugo Foscolo? The answer is that Goethe's *Werther* is incomparably superior to all its progeny. Despite its passages of intolerable sentimentality, it is richly endowed, in its structure, psychological penetration, its fresh, vigorous imagery and diction, with the attributes of greatness.

English Bibliography

Atkins, Stuart Pratt. "Johann Caspar Lavater and Goethe: Problems of Psychology and Theology in *Die Leiden des jungen Werthers*," PMLA 63 (1948), 520–576.
———. *The Testament of Werther in Poetry and Drama*, Cambridge, Mass., 1949.
Clark, R. T. Jr. "The Psychological Framework of Goethe's *Werther*," *The Journal of English and Germanic Philology* 46 (1947), 273–278.
Croce, Benedetto. *Goethe*, London, 1923.
Diez, Max. "The Principle of the Dominant Metaphor in Goethe's *Werther*," PMLA 51 (1936), 821–841; 985–1006.
Fairley, Barker. *A Study of Goethe*, Oxford, 1947.
Feuerlicht, Ignace. "Werther's Suicide: 'Instinct, Reason, and Defense,' " *German Quarterly*, 51 (1978), 476–489.
Goethe, Johann Wolfgang von. *Fiction and Truth*, Books 12 and 13.
Lange, Victor. "Goethe's Craft of Fiction," *Publication of the English Goethe Society*, N.S. 22 (1953), 31–63.
Long, O. W. "Werther in America," *Studies in Honor of John Albrecht Walz*, Lancaster, Pa., 1941.
Mann, Thomas. *The Beloved Returns*, 1940.
Maurois, André. *Werther*, in *Méipe*, 1926.
Rose, William. "The Historical Background of Goethe's *Werther*," in *Men, Myths and Movements in German Literature*, London, 1931.
Ryder, Frank (ed.). *George Ticknor's The Sorrows of Young Werther*, Chapel Hill, 1952.
Steinhauer, Harry. "Goethe's *Werther* After Two Centuries," *University of Toronto Quarterly*, 44 (No. 1, 1974) 1–13.
Strich, Fritz. *Goethe and World Literature*, London, 1949.
Viëtor, Karl. *Goethe the Poet*, Cambridge, Mass., 1949.
Wilkinson, Elizabeth M. and Willoughby, L. A. "The Blind Man and the Poet: An Early Stage in Goethe's Quest for Form." *Studies in Honor of L. H. Bruford*, London 1961, Pages 29–57.

German Bibliography

Beutler, Ernst. Introduction to Volume IV of the Artemis Goethe.

Chamberlain, Houston Stewart. *Goethe*, München, 1921.

Feise, Ernst. "Werther als nervöser Charakter," *The Germanic Review* I (1926), 185–253.

——. "Zu Entstehung, Problem und Technik von Goethes *Werther*," *The Journal of English and Germanic Philology* 13, (1914), 1–36.

Goethe, Johann Wolfgang von. *Dichtung und Wahrheit*, 12. und 13. Buch.

Gundolf, Friedrich. *Goethe*, Berlin, 1916.

Hermann, Max. Introduction to Volume VI of the Jubiläumsausgabe.

Kayser, Wolfgang. "Die Entstehung von Goethes *Werther*," *Deutsche Vierteljahrsschrift für Literaturwissenschaft und Geistesgeschichte* 19 (1941), 430–457.

Korff, H. A. *Geist der Goethezeit*. Vol. I, Leipzig, 1923.

Lange, Victor. "Die Sprache als Erzählform in Goethes *Werther*," *Formenwandel: Festschrift für Paul Böckmann*, (ed. Walter Müller-Seidel and Wolfgang Preisendanz) 261–272.

Ludwig, Emil. *Goethe*, Berlin, 1931.

Mann, Thomas. *Lotte in Weimar*, 1939.

——. "Goethes *Werther*," in *Altes und Neues*, Frankfurt a. M., 1953.

Meyer, Heinrich. *Goethe: Das Leben im Werk*, Hamburg, 1950.

Obenauer, Karl Justus. *Die Problematik des ästhetischen Menschen in der deutschen Literatur*, München, 1933.

Reiss, Hans. *Goethes Romane*, Bern, 1963.

Schöffler, Herbert. *Die Leiden des jungen Werther: Ihr geistesgeschichtlicher Hintergrund*, Frankfurt a. M., 1938.

Simmel, Georg. *Goethe*, Leipzig, 1921.

Staiger, Emil. *Goethe*. Vol. I, Zürich u. Freiburg, 1952.

Strich, Fritz. *Goethe und die Weltliteratur*, Bern, 1946.

Walzel, Oskar. Introduction to Volume IX of the Festausgabe.